LIKE MOTHER

Jenny Diski was born in 1947 in London where she
still lives.

'In *Like Mother*, the ideas of control, femininity and madness Diski explored with such calculated precision in her earlier novels are stretched tight around a structure which echoes and amplifies them. What's left is perhaps the bleakest and most powerful evocation of female nihilism in contemporary fiction. As a child, Frances is the mirror of her mother's desires, a polite little girl in a tutu and white gloves. But beyond the glass, she builds a shrine to badness, chanting 'fuck, fuck, fuck', revelling in its sound and her daring to defy adult taboos. Early on, the girl understands the principles of surveillance and secrecy. Just as her sexual experiments with the boy from the bombsite must be kept hidden, so 'White gloves were necessary *because* they were impossible to keep clean. It was white gloves dirtied that Ivy [her mother] looked for because they sat at the centre of the emotional web that tied life together.' Cultural symbols take on a terrifying resonance; gender is irrevocably inscribed in them. As her parents' blind and romantic marriage disintegrates, Frances resists by not caring, nurturing her private rage, fulfilling her desire for oblivion by breaking all the rules. *Like Mother* is brimful of ideas culled from psychoanalysis, structuralism and feminism. Yet Diski's novel defies neat definitions; she remains, as ever, sceptical of doctrines and givens . . . But if, as she suggests, the rules of gender difference fail, if language cannot contain or describe wretchedness, then what's the point of writing stories? Read this novel and you begin to understand.'

City Limits

'In Jenny Diski's novel the damage done by childhood pain seems more or less irreparable. *Like Mother* is the story of Frances, and her refusal to allow herself to care for anything once she deduced that happiness was never likely to be permanent. She has been crippled by her parents' disasterously quarrelsome marriage. A drab Fifties shortage of money is claustrophobically evoked, alongside a gentility in which her drunken mother advises: "A lady is never seen without her pair of gloves". Fortunately for the novel, Frances herself has a lively, wicked centre of her own which she preserves through most of the book, using schoolday naughtiness, experiments with sex and ether, and the lover who adores her equally ... Her tale is put into the imagined lips of her own brain-damaged baby, whose condition Frances approves as an image of her own pathological defence against hope. All this works much better than might be imagined, since for all her refusal to entertain hopes and fears, Frances is given a subversive honesty that is attractive.'

The Times

'Jenny Diski knows how to shock her readers, but she also knows how to train them in shock-absorption. The narrator of her latest novel is a baby without a brain – an anhydranencephalic, born with a maximum life expectancy of two years. Frances, her mother, calls the baby Nony (short for Nonentity). "An empty skull made sense to her" ... Like mother like daughter. Frances shares certain characteristics with her creator: a gift for discomforting those around her, an almost paranoid shrinking from sentimentality. You cannot fault Jenny Diski for the ease and originality of her writing. But her book remains disturbing, not least for the coolly observed suffering which haunts its pages ... Like a true modern, Jenny Diski exposes her own novel for the artifice it is. The reader is thus shielded from the disturbing impact of a powerful imagination.'

New Statesman

JENNY DISKI
LIKE MOTHER

V

VINTAGE

VINTAGE BOOK

20 Vauxhall Bridge Road, London SW1V 2SA

London Melbourne Sydney Auckland Johannesburg
and agencies throughout the world

First published by Bloomsbury Publishing Ltd., 1988
Vintage edition 1990

3 5 7 9 10 8 6 4 2

Printed and bound in Great Britain by
Cox & Wyman Ltd, Reading, Berks.

ISBN 0 09 966930 7

– Do you want to tell me something?
– No.

– Do you want to tell me something?
– No.

Do you want to tell me something?
– No.
– Well, we'll wait then. But I'm here to listen.

– Do you want to tell me something?
– Yes.
– Yes?
– I'll tell you a story to pass the time. About my mother. It's the only story I know.
– Go on. I'm listening.
– I know. What else is there for you to do?
– Sleep?
– I'd get lonely. You're here to listen.
– I know. I'm listening.
– You won't interrupt?
– I might, if there's something I don't understand. If I have a question.
– My mother's name was Frances. Are you ready for me to start the story?
– Go ahead.

FRANCES SAT OPPOSITE the Registrar while the baby lay in silence in her small pram.

'Nony Laughton.'

The Registrar looked up, his pen poised over the appropriate section of the birth certificate.

'Is that "N-o-n-n-y", as in "Hey, nonny nonny no"?' he smiled. He liked to think he had a humorous and amiable way of finding out the spelling of the more outlandish names. It wasn't for him to make judgements about what people called their kids.

Frances offered a small, dry smile in return.

'Something like that, but only one "n" in the middle.

'Right-oh. Nony Laughton, one "n" in the middle. Unusual name, that.'

Frances had explained the name to her daughter the previous evening.

'You're going to be called Nony. It's short for Nonentity. But that's just between you and me. It'll be our little joke.'

Frances had another pet name for the child that only the two of them knew about. She used it in the mornings when she woke her for the first feed of the day.

'And how's the Brainless Bastard this morning?' she'd yawn. 'Still with us, in your way?'

Frances watched her daughter's sightless eyes open as she put her to her breast. Sometimes her breathing was so light, and she was so still, that it was only when her eyes opened Frances could be sure she had survived the night. 'That's not fair though, is it?' she would say as Nony's sucking mechanism got started. 'It's only fifty per cent the truth. You *were* born in wedlock.'

– What was wrong with the baby?

– You said you wouldn't interrupt.

– I said I'd ask questions if I didn't understand. You want me to follow what you're saying, don't you?

– You're supposed to follow the thread of the narrative. You should listen more and talk less.

– But you said you would tell me the story of your mother. It didn't sound like the beginning of a story to me.

– It isn't. It's virtually the end. The mother dies and then the baby dies because of its impossible disabilities.

– What does the mother die of? What disabilities does the baby have? It's very difficult to follow a story that begins at the end. How can you have reached a conclusion when there's no beginning or middle?

– There is a beginning and a middle. It's just that you haven't heard them.

– Then you still have a story to tell. You aren't at the end.

– I am at the end if I know the rest of the story and the end is where I choose to start.

– Then what am I here for? Is it enough to tell a story that no one will listen to – that no one can understand?

– No. That's why you're here. All right, I'll tell you the rest, but I don't want to start right at the beginning yet.

– Do it your way. I'll listen.

FRANCES STEPPED OUT of the neon bright corridor, through the door, into the darkened room where, for a moment, she could see only the outline of three figures standing in a semicircle.

'Come in, Mrs Laughton. Please sit down.'

His voice was clipped and flat, with none of the usual melodious tones that eased people into rooms where others were already gathered. She could tell, although her eyes had still not yet adjusted to the darkness, that there was no smile on his face. The voice had an uncompromising finality. It was the voice of the headmaster interviewing the pupil who had finally gone too far, or the employer giving a persistent absentee his cards.

Frances tightened the muscles around her face and neck, steeling them so that the sound of his voice would bounce harmlessly off her.

She could see more clearly now. The three of them, the two nurses and the consultant in his white coat, stood against the drawn blinds. No one was smiling. In front of them was the perspex crib. She could hardly make out the small, still shape that lay inside. This was the first time she had seen it. She made a move towards the crib but stopped and turned abruptly towards a chair placed against the wall to her left.

'I think we had better just get on with it.' The consultant indicated to one of the nurses that she should pick up the baby.

The nurse held the infant against her breast, supporting the back of its head and neck in the palm of her hand. She turned to face the consultant so that Frances could see the baby's face rising above the nurse's shoulder.

Frances waited patiently, sitting very still and upright on the wooden chair. She felt some discomfort from the wound

11

in her abdomen and beneath that a subdued ache that suggested the painkillers were starting to wear off.

'The test we do in these cases is called transillumination. It's very simple and straightforward. Naturally, we did it immediately after the Caesarean, but I think you should see it for yourself.'

The other nurse stood like a shadow, with her hands folded in front of her, a little distance from Frances's chair. Her lips were pressed into a thin, tight line of disapproval.

The consultant switched on a torch that he had taken from the table behind him and held it against the back of the infant's skull. Frances didn't move a muscle. The beam from the torch glowed through the baby's translucent skull and lit up the limpid, sightless blue eyes like a Hallowe'en pumpkin. For a moment the room was silent as they all gazed at the illuminated head of the child. The baby's forehead glowed a pastel pink, like a nightlight in a child's room. But from the eyes poured cold bright beams as the light that was trapped and softened inside the watery skull found an exit.

Frances heard the nurse beside her draw in her breath. The paediatrician heard it too and switched off the torch.

'You can raise the blinds now,' he said to the nurse and nodded to the other one to replace the baby in the crib. 'Thank you,' he said in a quiet, but not unkindly, voice as the two uniformed women left the room.

The sudden brightness blinded Frances for a moment and she closed her eyes. Immediately an image formed on her lids, a negative of the glowing baby, darkness where the light had been, black holes for the illuminated eyes surrounded by the bright, curving outline of a baby's head. When she opened her eyes again the paediatrician was standing against the window, staring out across the skyline. He turned to look at Frances. He had expected shock, an emotional reaction. But her face showed nothing more than an attentive expectation that he was going to speak. She sat straight in the chair in a blue kimono-style dressing-gown, black ballet slippers on her feet. Her deep red hair lacked the sheen it had when washed regularly, but retained its own internal glow. It was pulled back, tidily, away from her face, the bulk of it clipped at the back. She was pale still from the anaesthetic, but her face was composed. There was even a hint of a polite smile. The doctor dismissed the momentary thought of comfort that had flitted across his mind as he stared out of the window. Frances spoke first.

'So the tests were right, then?'

'There was always a very high chance that they would be. There wasn't any doubt that there would be severe brain-damage.' He sounded like a man assuring her of his clear conscience. Frances answered him with equal confidence.

'I know. I'd like to know what the situation is, please.'

'As you saw, there are no cerebral hemispheres. The light shines through because there's nothing to stop it. No brain, at least not in any human sense. As you know, when we discussed this after the amniocentesis, I expected the baby to be born without cerebral hemispheres, but there was always the chance that the lower brain would be intact, and that has turned out to be the case. Which is why it has survived. The autonomic system is functioning; it can breathe, eat, maintain its temperature, digest, excrete, everything any living organism has to do to stay alive. But it cannot hear, feel, or see. It won't ever think or experience anything.'

His voice remained cold and clinical, the details clear and crisp. He's punishing me, Frances thought, he's punishing me with reality.

He continued.

'Infants born in this condition are called anhydranence-phalics. It means that there is water where the cerebral hemi-spheres should be. The mid-brain, basal ganglia and cerebel-lum are in place and functioning. In the old days, before we could test for it,' and here there was a slight pause, 'babies in this condition *were* occasionally born. We know that those that survive birth can stay alive for a while but they generally succumb quite soon to infections that prove fatal. I can't say how long – weeks, months, perhaps. Two years is the longest any anhydranencephalic has been known to survive.'

Frances kept her eyes squarely on him as he spoke, her hands folded in her lap. When it was clear he had finished she said, 'Thank you. She doesn't have to stay in hospital then?'

'There's nothing we can do for the child. There is no prognosis, Mrs Laughton.'

'Thank you,' Frances repeated.

'If you'll excuse me . . . I have to get to my next appointment. The nurse will return the baby to the nursery when you're ready.'

At the door he stopped and turned back towards Frances. The mask of indifference remained on his face, but thinned all of a sudden like stretched skin, so that Frances could perceive the anger concealed beneath it. But this too was no more than a camouflaging layer. It was as if she were looking at an X-ray. She peered into his face and saw, behind the anger and indifference, the skeleton of perplexity.

'Why . . . ?' he began. But instantly the anger and distance returned, snapping his face shut. He left the room without another word, closing the door on Frances, and re-entered the evenly lit world of the hospital where anxious parents waited for him to offer hope of recovery and repair.

Frances got up and walked over to the baby in the crib. She stood for a moment, looking down at it.

The baby looked perfectly normal; better, in fact, than most of the other babies she had seen being carried up and down the corridor from her side room off the post-natal ward. Caesarean babies made an easy entrance into the world and didn't come out looking so squeezed. Frances had to remind herself of what she had just seen. But the baby did lie strangely still. Frances reached into the crib and stroked the tiny head, running her palm across the wispy strands of new-born hair. It was a pale rust colour. She'll have my hair, Frances thought. The baby continued to lie passively, blue eyes open, but static and unfocused, not seeing and so not looking.

Frances smiled an easy smile.

'Hello you.' She spoke softly but conversationally. 'We're both in disgrace. That's a hell of a way to start life, isn't it? In trouble. Never mind, you won't have to worry about what people say, because you won't hear them, will you? But I'll

14

tell you something,' Frances lowered her voice, speaking now in a conspiratorial whisper to her blind, deaf and terminal baby. 'We're very lucky, you and I. We won't ever be a disappointment to each other.'

– If the baby has no higher brain function, and you are the baby, how can you be telling me this story?

– Pardon?

– You wouldn't have any language. You couldn't think. You'd be living in a silent, hermetically sealed universe. What would I be doing here? How could you tell me the story of your mother, or anything at all?

– I told you at the beginning I didn't have anything to tell you.

– You couldn't have told me that without a brain.

– I didn't.

– I heard it, though, and everything else you've said.

– That's because you're here to listen.

– It's hard to follow your line of reasoning.

– You're making this very difficult and that's not what you're here for. Do you have to have an explanation for everything?

– No, but it would help me make sense of what I hear.

– You seem to have a great commitment to logic. It will make demands on me as a storyteller. I don't know if I'm up to it. I could just lie here in the dark listening to the silence.

– Except that you want to tell me the story of your mother.

– I want to pass the time. I have nothing but the story of my mother to tell. I'll try and explain, if I must. I have a gift to compensate for my empty skull.

– A gift?

– Knowledge of my mother. Not thought, not language. Blood knowledge. Genetic information. Blind, dumb, know-nothing kid I may be, but I have the whole story of my mother, all the knowledge I need to make the story, floating about in the watery spaces inside my skull. It's a kind of perception, if you don't take it in its narrowest sense.

– But still, I don't see how you can *tell* the story to someone else.

– What else can you do with a story? I grant it may not be the most useful gift I could have been given but, since I've got it, I thought I might as well make use of it. As I said, to pass the time.

– So?

– So that's what you're for. To listen to my mother's story.

– To listen to a story without words?

– To listen to a story told in imagined words. And who better to hear such a story than an imagined listener?

– I'm your creation, then?

– I don't want to argue about it. My blood circulates, my heart beats. The ancient brain at the top of my spinal column keeps me functioning. To the world out there I'm just one of Nature's jokes – the apotheosis of developmental evolution with the brain of a salamander. But maybe there's more to me than meets the crude and fearful gaze of those who rate their cerebral hemispheres so highly.

– Such as the capacity to invent a story, a language, and a listener to hear it?

– I'd shrug if I could. Sometimes, in the early evening, Mother sat on the floor beside my cot, watching the light fade. One night, as she was lighting a cigarette – there was no need for her to be careful of my young lungs – she held the lighter up to the window – it was translucent – and saw that it was empty.

– You seem to have changed to first person. Is this part of the story?

– No. It's part of the explanation. Shall I go on?

– OK.

– Mother flicked the wheel that made the spark and held it out to me as the flame sprang up. 'Look, Nony,' she said, 'there's nothing in it. It's empty. The sparks are lighting just from the memory of the gas.' Maybe she had something. Perhaps, in the clear liquid that sloshes around behind my blind eyes, there's some residue of humanity that wants to make a story. People have to explain, they have to try and make sense of things. Even me, maybe. I need you if I am to

17

give the blindsight a shape. I have to have someone who can listen to the language I don't have. I need you to imagine the world I have no commerce with.

– All right. That sounds like a reasonable basis for my existence. If you need me to listen to your story, I'm here.

– You haven't got any choice, you smug bastard. You're a captive audience.

– If you could see me I'd smile noncommittally at you. Why don't you go on with your story?

– My mother's story.

– Yes, that.

– Well, it wasn't me that interrupted. If you've got the situation straight now, I'll get on with it.

FRANCES DIDN'T HUM lullabies to her daughter at bedtime, or prod her teasingly where her umbilicus once was
when she changed her dirty nappy. She didn't throw her
infant in the air, to thrill her and reassure her that she would
always be caught safely in her arms. She did talk to her
sometimes, telling her things, though with the half-distracted
look in her eye of someone who was really talking to themselves. But Frances was a good mother and she didn't fuss.

Nony couldn't charm or irritate her way to food. She was
fed at regular intervals, according to the clock, not because
she had enticed the breast from its covering with dimples or
whines. But she could suck and feel hunger pangs like any
other baby. When the time came she drew the food from the
nipple until she was full while Frances held her steady in the
crook of her arm. It was their moment of physical contact,
although at the beginning Frances was quite cautious about
fondling the child. But Nony was warm and soft and her
heart beat like other babies and Frances derived some physical pleasure from those moments.

With the bath and nappy changing, things weren't quite
the same. Frances performed the tasks but Nony's body
always lay so unnaturally still that nothing more than
Frances's hands were involved. Nony was immobile as
Frances clasped the tiny ankles together in her fist and raised
them to wipe and dry and powder her anus and vagina.

Occasionally the baby went into spasm, drawing her knees
stiffly to her chest, her arms tensed and bent at the elbow. It
looked awkward, but Frances knew the infant felt nothing
and that there was no cause for special concern. The rest of
the time Nony lay still on her back or her stomach as she
had been placed.

At least to the naked eye Nony was a perfect-looking

19

specimen of her sex. Her reproductive organs were intact. Her vagina was a hairless mound, enlarged, like all new-born females, with the residue of her mother's oestrogen, the clitoris protruding like a baby bird's beak, pinkly from its nest. But when Frances's fingers brushed against it, or her nappy rubbed, she didn't feel that tingling, unidentifiable hunger that other, normal, girl children feel. 'You need brains to appreciate sex. You're living proof of that,' Frances told her, adding, 'if you can call it living.'

Again, like all new-born females, Nony had a tiny uterus and the egg sacs at the entrance to her Fallopian tubes contained a reproductive lifetime's worth of ova. If she could have reached menses, one egg each month would ripen and prepare itself for fertilization. They were all there, ready and waiting pointlessly for their turn. 'Just as well,' Frances said briskly. 'We don't want too many of your kind around.'

But, for all the sexual equipment, there was nothing that could be called girlish about Nony. Frances supposed that gender was all in the brain, like sex.

Sometimes Frances wondered if there wasn't something of the world that impinged, like a distant star in an endless universe, on the absolute blackness and silence of her existence. There was no hope in the thought. Frances had none, wanted none. She only wondered. She knew Nony for what she was. My little girl, Frances smiled. She was nothing if not a realist. Nony had, after all, been chosen. She was no unstoppable accident.

No one understood why Frances had refused to abort the foetus, and she did nothing to help them. If she had offered any explanation at all, some people might have forgiven her. She could have said she had suffered a sudden religious conversion, or that she was, by the time of the amniocentesis, biologically bonded to the foetus inside her, defective or not. She might have claimed to be grasping the remote chance that the test was wrong, or offered a neurotic but understandable revulsion against going through a labour to produce a dead foetus. Anything of that kind might have quietened the anger and opposition by providing a small bridge of reason for people to cross.

But she said nothing. She smiled and shrugged and remained implacable. She frightened people with that.

There *were* some people who did feel that there was something indefinable in the normal foetus that had a claim on life. Those who, while not condemning abortion for others, would have rejected it themselves. But even those people found their ethical objections inapplicable in this case. The thing Frances had inside her was in no recognizable sense human, and no human ethical stance seemed relevant to it.

The rationalists, the medical world and the professional carers told Frances she was irresponsible and selfish. She agreed quietly to the accusation of selfishness, but couldn't see to whom she was being irresponsible. When her husband was mentioned, Frances nodded comprehension and said, 'Oh, yes.'

No one could find Frances's decision other than reprehensible. She didn't, being the person she was, make much effort to explain herself, but even if she had she would have been condemned. People simply couldn't understand. They were only human, and anyone in possession of the grey matter that makes people only human, connected to each other by learning, tradition and need, would feel the same.

When the result of the test was through, Frances, twenty-two weeks pregnant, sat, with her husband, in the consultant's office listening to his tactful diagnosis.

'The foetus is incomplete, I'm afraid. Under the circumstances an abortion would be advisable. There's only the remotest chance that the foetus is viable. Better to try again.'

Frances wasn't to be satisfied with that.

'What, exactly, do you mean by "incomplete"?'

The consultant gave them the details regretfully, knowing that, in these cases, it was better if the details were fudged.

Her husband dropped his head into one hand and reached for Frances's with the other. He hadn't wanted to hear all the details. Frances let his hand lie limp on top of hers.

'How soon can the . . . termination be arranged?' he asked, squeezing her fingers together.

'Immediately. Within the next day or two. It's not a good idea to wait.'

21

Frances stood up. The bulge was already evident.

'Thank you,' she said to the consultant. 'But I'll go through with the pregnancy. And, if the baby lives, I'd appreciate it if you'd tell the midwife not to pinch its nose, or whatever they do to despatch them. Incidentally, the amniocentesis must have shown the sex. Boy or girl?'

The man beside her jumped from his chair and closed in on her.

'Frances! You aren't serious?'

'Boy or girl?' Frances repeated.

The consultant looked at her thoughtfully. 'We don't usually give parents that information. It's policy.'

'I know everything else about the child. There's not much point in keeping its sex a secret, is there?'

'Mrs Laughton, you're very understandably upset. You need some time to adjust. I know how terrible a thing this is to come to terms with. We have a counsellor who can help. Mr Laughton, perhaps you would give me a ring later this afternoon and we can arrange an appointment for both of you?' He gave the other man a look that Frances was not supposed to see, being too distracted.

'The sex, please,' Frances demanded firmly, seeing but choosing to ignore the look.

'It's female, Mrs Laughton.'

'Thank you,' said Frances and left the room, her long back straight, her head high and perfectly centred over her spine. Her husband followed her out of the room numbly.

He found Frances's decision as unintelligible and offensive as everyone else did. He had a more conventional view of existence than Frances and expected babies to come complete and ready to grow in the time-honoured way. Although he had had occasion to enjoy his wife's curiously dry sense of humour, he discovered there were limits to his ability to appreciate it.

'Well, nobody's perfect,' Frances shrugged when they got home after the interview. She turned her long green eyes on him and offered to share a smile. Frances's smiles were emporia. A complete selection of shades of meaning flickered around the stretched muscles of her mouth and eyes, from the black bleakness of despair, to the palest pastel wash of frivolity. It was for the observer to choose from what was on offer.

But he had reached his threshold. There were some things he felt unable to smile about. He didn't have Frances's range.

'For God's sake, Frances!'

And, although Frances had a ready answer to that, she said no more than, 'Mmm . . .' in reply.

– Your mother sounds an unusual woman.

– She was. She was remarkable.

– Why did she react like that?

– Because that was how she felt. An empty skull made sense to her.

– But why did she feel like that?

– She just did. That's how she was. Why do you have to ask why all the time?

– Because you've got me interested. If you begin at the end of a story, it's only natural that your listener will want to know how it began.

– You sound like my mother's English teacher.

– How's that?

– Mother became a writer, you know. She wrote short stories. That was after she stopped being a dancer and was pregnant with me.

– You do jump about. I wish you would get to the beginning of the story.

– I will, eventually. Just be patient. What else is there for you to do? I hate stories. The beginnings, the middles, the ends. That's what the English teacher said to Mother. Stories have to have beginnings, middles and ends. Mother's stories didn't work like that; they started nowhere and ended in the same place. You see, I am my mother's daughter, in some ways I take after her.

– Yes.

– That was the title of one of the stories in her only collection – 'From Nowhere to Nowhere'. Mother said that life didn't have a beginning, middle and end. It just went on and stopped where it felt like it, and hardly ever made sense. But her teacher explained that stories weren't supposed to be like life. They were crafted; contrivances to keep readers involved.

– She had a point.

– Miss Barnes, her teacher, was particularly keen on the short-story form. 'The story must carry the reader with it,' she told Mother. 'It must pick you up right at the start and then provide little peaks of excitement that keep you interested and wanting more, wanting to go on, to get to the end, so you can say: "Aah, so that's what happened, and that's why it happened." '

– She had a point. Speaking as a listener, I can't disagree with Miss Barnes.

– Mother certainly agreed that that didn't sound much like life. And I agree with her. *I* think stories are gaolers. They make both the teller and the listener their prisoner, incarcerated by the requirements of the narrative, by the need for a coherent explanation. I didn't invent you so that I could give you an explanation of Mother, I just wanted to tell you who she was. I don't want to construct a pile of events that assume more importance than the life itself. Stories have a life of their own. And look what's happened already. Now there are three of us. You, me, and the story. Like a monstrous, demanding child, it needs feeding with motivation and consequence. And what else can I do, whiling away the time, but feed the greedy, bastard story? I wish I hadn't started. I wish there was no beginning, no middle, no . . .

– End. What would you do instead?

– I would be content with timelessness. With being nothing waiting for nothing. A heaviness has come over me, around my chest and heart. Brainlessness doesn't save me from it. It's the weight of incident bearing down on me, I think. An empty world cluttered with events I have to shape and make sense of simply because I allowed another into my solitude. If I hadn't invented you I'd be more myself, free from the burden of your demands for a coherent story. Perhaps I made a mistake in thinking that I needed words to pass the time; I may have been better off without them, and you.

– Why not take a rest for a moment? There's no hurry.

– A passing cloud. A dark moment. I feel better now. Mother had those moments too. That's when she wrote her stories.

– What were they like, her stories?

– There was one that became a kind of bedtime story, special to us. Mother often read it to me when her spirits were low.

– But you couldn't hear it?

– Well, not in the sense you mean. But I know it.

– I'd like to hear it.

– It was called 'Slime Mold'. When her agent read it, she said, 'That's not a short story. It's biology – of the worst kind.' So Mother included it in the collection, and called the whole volume *Biology of the Worst Kind*. It's very short. This is it.

SLIME MOLD

Slime molds live in the soil of this planet. As many as a billion of them exist in just one square foot of earth. This is because they are very small.

The problem about slime molds is that it's very hard to decide if they are plants or animals. To overcome this ambiguity, Haeckel, the German taxonomist, invented the term *protista*, which was supposed to designate them a separate category from *plantae* and *animalia*. But this was merely a cunning device to prevent people from spending too much time worrying about the real problem that remained and remains unsolved: are slime molds creatures or things? The answer is that they are neither and both. But it's upsetting.

When slime molds (of which there are as many as five hundred varieties) begin their life cycle they veer towards being a lower order of plant, at the fungal end of life. But we don't expect much of fungi, so slime molds surprise us. Later, when they aggregate, creep and feed, they are more like animals. They *do* things, like go about in gangs.

To begin with there are just single-celled amoeba, which, like many forms of individual life, repel each other. They lead a solitary existence and manage very well on their own until food gets short. Then, instead of just quietly starving to death, they start to move, just a few at first, but all in the same direction, left or right, one or the other. The cells in the front, the advance guard, produce a substance that stimulates others to follow and join. Repulsion is replaced by the herd instinct, until, finally, a great migration occurs and the cells all meet and swarm. Then there are no more individual cells; the slime mold has become a single shape that moves and looks exactly like a slug. You'd mistake it for a slug (a small one, only half an inch long) if you saw it, but actually it's one hundred thousand cells agreeing to do the same thing. More like an animal grazing.

Now the slug begins to change. Stalks develop with tiny spores at the tip and their translucent colour changes through purple to black. Then the stalk contracts, squeezing its substance into the head until it explodes spores into the soil, each becoming a single-celled amoeba-like thing that manages very well on its own, thank you.

The life cycle of the slime mold takes place within twenty hours. Longevity is not a characteristic of this species.

All this may seem very purposeful. It's certainly very complicated. But there's not a whit of intention about any of it. Scientists are quite clear that the whole devious business comes about because the single cells produce a substance called cyclic adenosine monophosphate. An enzyme, I think. It's got nothing to do with wanting anything.

I read about slime molds in my local library in the *Encyclopaedia Britannica*. They were under the main heading '*Protozoans*'. The next part of the article concerned more developed forms of life and began: 'Much of the beauty and diversity of contemporary life on Earth is due to sex.'

– Is that it?
– Yes. Mother dedicated *Biology of the Worst Kind* to me. On the first blank page it says:

> To Nony,
> who understands the nature and existence
> of slime molds like no one else.

– That must have made you very proud. I can see why you like the story. Do you feel ready to tell me about Frances now?
– All right. From the beginning?

– That's how I'd like to hear it.

– You mean my mother's beginnings?

– Is there any better way of describing who a person is?

– You mean childhood, background, that kind of thing? The arbitrary reproductive arrangements that determine character?

– That has to be an important part, doesn't it? A mixture of biology and history?

– The public and private cage of being?

– You're very cynical for one so young.

– I'm not your usual kind of youngster. Anyway, biology is my mistress, I dance to her tune alone. And, to tell you the truth, I'm not sure I could put my hand on my vigorous little heart and say I'm sorry about that. Not when you look at the alternative.

– Your mother's story, you mean? Tell me. I'm listening.

– If I had anything between my ears, I could dream instead of having to dance to your tune. Dreaming must be fun. A way of telling a story to yourself without having to make sense, because there's no one else there. The story the dreamer dreams can be told in its own way, in its own order. I resent your needs, but I suppose that's no more than saying I resent my need for you. If I could dream I'd be the dance itself, I'd have no need of dancer or choreography.

– But look at the price people have to pay for dreams. Look at all the reality they have to get through before they can spend a few hours alone, inside themselves.

– You're right, I've got a lot to be grateful for. From the beginning then?

– Why not? It'll pass the time.

IVY AND GERALD Pepper found the war very much to their liking.

They married on the day that Neville Chamberlain came down the steps of his aircraft flapping a piece of paper in the breeze. Ivy sat side-saddle on Gerald's lap, her smart black hat still perched on top of her carefully arranged waves, while they listened to the radio news.

'Well, I've got my piece in my time, too. Right here and now,' Gerald chuckled into Ivy's ear, sliding his hand under her tight skirt and up beyond the top of her stocking to squeeze the ample, soft flesh of her inner thigh. Ivy giggled and wriggled just enough to cause her legs to spread a little wider and her full bosom to compress against Gerald's jacket.

'And I've got *my* piece of paper to make sure it stays that way,' he added, nuzzling her ear and walking two fingers of the hand beneath her skirt higher up her thigh.

'Here we are then,' he said when the fingers had arrived at their destination. He reached round her neck with his spare arm into the opening of her blouse and grabbed more than a handful of weighty, satin-covered breast. 'All mine. Signed, sealed and delivered. Come on, then, girl. Lie down and deliver.'

Ivy pressed her face against Gerald's cheek, engulfing him in the sweet scent of face powder. 'You naughty, dirty thing,' she lisped before probing his ear with the moist, lipstick-smudged tip of her tongue.

The jovial innocence of this scene had more to do with the atmosphere of a world perched uncertainly between war and peace, sitting side-saddle on the lap of catastrophe, than with the character and experience of Ivy and Gerald themselves. They were neither as young nor as fresh as their behaviour suggested, though they had just come from the registry office and Gerald's red carnation smelt as sweet as virginity.

They were in their late thirties, and for both of them this was a second marriage. Gerald's previous dismal and mutually adulterous marriage had finally come to an end when his young son had run out of the house to escape the roars of recrimination, straight into an oncoming car. Ivy's first husband had come home from a business trip to find her swaying drunkenly in Gerald's arms to the smooth tones of Sam Costa. Gerald was new to him, but 'Sam's Song' and the drunken swaying weren't, and he had handed her over to Gerald with such evident relief that Gerald had wondered whether it wouldn't be worth asking for a few quid into the bargain. In the end he settled for the small flat in the centre of London that husband number one was pleased enough to see the back of.

But they were still an attractive pair and neither of them had any other plans. Gerald's glossy, film-star good looks and smoothed-back hair gave him a glamour that had only the merest hint of shadiness about it, and Ivy was still plumply pretty, round and girlishly coy. In spite of the equality of their years, Gerald liked that; it made him feel she needed looking after. Gerald needed, Ivy knew, her comfort for the lost son.

Perhaps innocence isn't, after all, such an inappropriate description of the pair of them then. Neither of them knew what they were doing. Wiser people, watching from a distance, might have shaken their heads sorrowfully as they saw the couple seal their fate at the registry office, their future as plain and visible as their past, but utterly concealed from the two of them, adding their signatures to the marriage register. His, an impressive but indecipherable flourish, hers, the careful round hand of the elementary school.

But the times colluded with those who could not see, rather than those who could. The wind fluttered the optimism that people grasped between their fingers and made it look alive. Only some knew, and few said, that wishes weren't enough, that how things *had* been affected how things were to be, and that nothing is ever just going to be all right now, simply because we want it so.

Gerald and Ivy knew, vaguely, of stories that, even when known only vaguely, chilled the blood. There were rumours going around the East End communities that they now only visited, that spoke of cattle trucks and their human cargo, whose destinations were unknown but guessed at. When things looked bad for the Allies, Ivy and Gerald became uncomfortably half-aware that very few miles and mere fortune separated them from the worst that human beings could do. They were both born Londoners, after all, because ghettos and pogroms were nothing new. But this was never spoken of between them, perhaps never even consciously thought. In spite of the sound of Mosley's voice still echoing through the streets of the East End; in spite of Gerald having changed his name before the war from Israel Pfeiffer because 'it would be better for business'; and despite the narrowness of the English Channel, Ivy and Gerald felt remote from the fate of the European Jews. They felt so *English*, they had done so well in a land where their fathers were still foreigners with broken accents. Gerald and Ivy could feel pity for the victims, and hatred for their persecutors, but no real connection. If they trembled at the possibility of a German victory they were never fully conscious of why they did so.

They both put poverty and foreignness behind them. The war had launched them into the bravado of blitz society and they were pleased with how life was going. Neither of them relished visiting their parents, old people uprooted from old countries and never quite at ease in England. They severed their connections gradually but firmly, detaching themselves as they told each other how successful they had been in achieving their parents' ambitions for them. Thanks to Gerald's dealings on the black market they had money and what money could buy, and a circle of friends who hovered on the fringes of show business and society. They were integrated and successful, what more could their parents want? And, if Gerald had not become the scholar his father had hoped for, he had gained enough of an education to be able to convince his business contacts that he knew his way around and was almost just like them.

They had known hard childhoods, failed marriages, but, as the war came to a successful conclusion, it seemed to Ivy and Gerald that they had won through too. They were conscious every day that these were the good times they had been waiting for. Gerald and Ivy were not culpable, not cruel, only a little stupid and thoughtless. For them the past was over and done with, and the future a straight, uncomplicated path from the present. Generation after generation.

– Your grandparents?

– Yes. Granny and Grandpa. Is that the sort of beginning you had in mind? Frances's story began like everyone's before her time. Of course, Granny and Grandpa were no more than the consequences of other people's lives and earlier history. Shall I start again with Great-Granny and Great-Grandpa?

– You might as well begin with the Big Bang.

– You have a point. Where else is there to begin? If it's a real story you want, with a beginning, middle and end . . .

– We probably don't have the time.

– You're right, let's be practical.

IVY AND GERALD danced in the streets with the rest of London on VE night, swaying and singing amid the laughing thousands who repossessed the night-time city. Their voices joined the great wave of sound that rose to cheer the blatant, blazing anti-aircraft searchlights, the beams racing and inter-weaving in the dark sky as if to signal to the universe that all was well down here again.

They walked home unsteadily in the early hours, leaning against each other for warmth and stability. Gerald stopped and wrapped his jacket around Ivy's naked shoulders, pulling her towards him by the lapels.

'What about a baby then, old girl?' He rested his forehead against Ivy's and they rocked gently back and forth while their alcohol-slow brains turned the sound of his words into meaning.

Ivy's sleepy, dazed eyes focused suddenly in alarm. Some-where at the back of her mind she had known it would come, this question, but the flashing image she had now, of pain, and the sound in her inner ear of a baby screaming for attention, made her eyes sharp with astonishment and horror for a second. Then the picture changed and she saw a uniformed nanny pushing an imposing baby carriage (there was one she had seen advertised as the Rolls-Royce of peram-bulators, she remembered) containing a smiling, sleeping, heartbreakingly pretty child, dressed in the finest the black market could provide.

'A son, you know . . .' He glanced down at Ivy to see if she was catching his drift, and saw her eyes soft and misty with pleasure. But the contents of her splendid perambulator were all pink: blankets, bootees, bonnet. Later there would be diminutive ballet shoes, a tiny tutu, gala birthday parties with tiered cakes. Pink, pink, everything, sugar pink. She blinked up at Gerald.

'Mmm . . .' she smiled, sleepy, drunk and dreamy. 'Yes, a baby.'

And anyway, they both thought, as they neared the flat, they had to round off their victory night celebrations somehow.

Wiser eyes, if they had been watching, would have seen the distance between Ivy and Gerald's dreams, and the even greater distance between either of their dreams and reality. The eyes, most likely, would have turned away to avoid the pain of seeing what they could do nothing about. If anyone had been watching, what could they have said? *'The two of you and the world are not as they seem to you to be. You are not qualified; you are not fit to raise a new member of the human race without pain and sorrow for you all'*? But there are no qualifications needed, and half the world had just fought and won a righteous war against the other half, to ensure that that was the case. Ivy and Gerald would conceive a dream and face reality nine months later. They were not unusual. Wisdom would have kept the watchers silent, but, in any case, no one *was* watching.

And so Frances was conceived from a lusty, amiable, drunken coupling, on a night when the world, or most of it, had something to celebrate.

Frances Pepper was one of 955,000 new babies that Britain welcomed to its landmass in 1946. Their birth coincided with the worst winter Britain had known this century. There was not to be another like it until 1962. But in spite of the snow and frozen pipes the women of post-war Britain were swollen with a generation that was born in a caul of optimism. Frances grew up in a post-war Britain where the reality of the word 'austerity' paced side by side with a sense of future born out of the immediate past. The air was filled with stories of history only just made: the heroic oratory of Churchill; villains defeated and, at Nuremberg, punished; heroes and heroines of the Resistance. The children received these stories along with – as part of – the creation myths of their culture and time, bedrock on which a sunny future would be built. They were simple tales of good and evil, as uncomplicated as their narrators.

To Frances, in her earliest years, the story of how the world was now and how it had been was something of an abstraction, coming from the distant times, like the stories of Genesis, or Sleeping Beauty, or the primeval soup. Two years or five hundred million had the same remote, mythological quality of being before her entry on to the planet. But still, it was clear to most of the children that they had arrived at just the right time, when everything was all right again, though, of necessity, a little short, temporarily, on supplies. They were comforted to find themselves in a world where good had already triumphed, as if they had moved into a new house that had been redecorated for their arrival.

Frances and her contemporaries grew with the feeling that they had been born in the aftermath of history. History had happened for some years prior to their birth when great events had occurred and great figures stalked the earth. Some were still alive, others dead, but they were all ghosts to the children of 1946. History was over, the deeds had been done; good and bad, war and genocide, statesmanship and pragmatism, danger and excitement. They were now stories to be told, lessons to be learned. They had come after; their conception in such unprecedented numbers, a very signal that history had finished, and the world returned to what it must once have been: a march of uneventful days, a simple progression from now onwards that required peopling. A dark night had been followed inevitably by the dawn which, just as inevitably, would grow brighter. A bit of bad weather that year could hardly shake the stronger pattern that had been etched into the growing tendrils of their brains.

It may have been that there were wiser people somewhere, who watched events with a greater sense of distance, and felt that, on the contrary, the temporary bumps and slides of what was called history, for all their excitement, were less of a story to tell the children than the endless sweep of the universe, the greater patterns of geological time and events.

And that a bad winter on a tiny northern island told a deeper tale. Should the new generation know the nature of the place in which they found themselves, or the nature of the people they found themselves with? Ideally, both should be known, no question of that; but which story do you tell first? Which explains more to the empty, questioning intelligence that has to inhabit the planet? But few of the children got to meet those wiser people, and most of the storytellers were not aware that there was more than one tale to tell.

So the weather took a back-seat, a practical background of how many blankets should be on the pram during the daily walk, and the world emerged as a roller-coaster of human doings, at rest after a particularly bumpy ride.

But the world didn't recover overnight from the binge of a world war. The hangover kept thrift and patience high on the list of desirable qualities. The war was won, but still little Frances in her pram watched her mother tear the perforations of the ration book at the butcher, and observed the flourish with which she presented her with her daily breakfast egg. It was one of the world's mysteries to Frances that a thing so shiny white could only be obtained from the Black Market. But this place, she learned, was the source of all the most desirable things in life. She imagined a pitch-black cavern, lit only by the inner light that glowed from the objects for sale. The secret shoppers found their way by the light of new-laid eggs, nylon stockings, bars of chocolate, to their heart's desire and when there, most astonishing of all apparently, paid only *money* for it. She longed to visit, seeing in her mind all the exotic creatures her story books described; Eastern potentates, wily merchants, kohl-eyed dancing girls dressed in wisps of material spun from sugar and gold thread. But she only ever got to visit the butcher and the ironmonger's shop, where ration coupons were carefully separated by a licked finger and handed over with far more reluctance than the pennies and half-crowns.

And there was the weather. After the snow and ice which kept the infant Frances bundled in layer upon layer of scratchy wool, the spring arrived. Rivers thawed and rain poured in unprecedented quantities throughout the summer. The rivers burst their banks and filled the newspapers with photographs of Mum and Dad, Gran and the kids sitting on the roof with a few pathetic treasures saved from the floodwaters that lapped at the eaves.

In reality they were grim days, and people could be heard to mutter, 'Is this what we won the war for?' And yet it didn't stop the stories that rode into the children's consciousness on the currents of air, telling them that the world had recovered from something and that everything was going to be all right now.

It was really no one's fault that most of the children of the post-war bulge would believe all their lives in happy endings and in the inevitable triumph of good over evil. Even when later events in the world and in their lives proved their early experience wrong, it was rarely quite wrong enough to overcome that initial training in hope. For many of them, nothing went terribly awry, and the glory that seemed part of those unspoken promises remained; admittedly never quite achieved, always just a little ahead of where they had got to, but never definitely off the agenda of their lives.

For Frances, though, history didn't impinge with quite the same intensity as it did for many. It was there, that sense of living in an historical watershed, but her private world, the one she lived and breathed daily, was too strong to allow her to pay very much attention to outside events.

The infant Frances (container of a highly dubious ovum, quite possibly) was the very stuff of Ivy Pepper's dreams. She lay wide-eyed in her crib, absorbing the sound of human voices and the shape of the world; a quiet, watchful, touchingly serious baby swaddled in pink blankets. By the time she was a few weeks old she had learned to distinguish the undulating cadences of the sound that would one day be language to her. The drone from a distance: a deep sound alternating with a series of lighter notes, the ebb and flow of conversation between Gerald and Ivy in the next room. An increase in volume and steep rise in pitch always preceded a face looming over her cot, its lips pursing and stretching to push the sing-song, melodic sound towards her. The faces chirruped and trilled at her, all of it meaningless but vital as milk.

When Frances had no sounds to listen to, or when she tired of listening, she looked. The still baby-blue eyes gazed long and hard at whatever was in their line of vision, making a cool appraisal of the environment. When her head rolled accidentally, first this way, then that, her eyes took advantage of the change of view to assess what kind of place she was in. She absorbed the geometry of the world from her immediate, limited surroundings. But everything she needed to accomplish the task was close at hand.

The shapes and angles of the room were embedded into her developing synapses as a spatial paradigm for the pattern of the planet. There were the straight and parallel lines of the walls and slats of her cot, the right-angles where horizontal met vertical at ceiling, on her cot, in doorways and windows. Above and to her left hung the spherical lampshade, a plain circle when dark, but deepened to three dimensions when alight. On the walls were pictures of stylised but representative human and animal forms, made up from shapes she recognised from the room itself. Hung above her cot was a string of less naturally occurring shapes – triangles, stars, hexagons – that the adults fidgeted to attract her attention when they came to stand over her and coo. Everything that was not her was the precise and definite shape of Euclidean geometry. Everything that was her prepared her for a world occupied predominantly by human beings. If she had been born with the capacity to perceive any other arrangement of shape in space, the weeks of passive looking submerged it and brought her into this world, and this world only.

It was necessary, of course, because by the time she was ready to walk, she had to know how not to bump into the world. What was submerged had to stay that way, squeezing into corners of herself until dream or reverie made space for it briefly to emerge. Even then language had done its job, and the strange arrangements she thought she almost saw were so bereft of words that they couldn't be remembered by a brain that had had phonetics burned into it in its first year, and then the meaning that accompanied the sound, so that by the time she was a couple of years old it was clear exactly what was thinkable and what not. She learned, through toys and games and example, to begin with the concrete and material at all times, so that the pattern of the concrete became the very pattern of her cerebral hemispheres. Frances learned as part of the process of learning the elementary limitations of thought and perception from her elders and betters. And with that she became a fit and proper member of her species.

She was what Ivy called a *good* baby. She cried very little, and this too was something she had to learn. A new human creature with a complete brain but no language of its own has nothing to rely on but its sensitivity to external stimuli and response. Frances learned very quickly that crying evoked responses that were not pleasing to her. The body that brought the bottle was usually Ivy's and had its own familiar smell and feel that comforted, but there were detectable differences in it if it arrived in response to Frances's cries. The skin felt cooler against her own, almost chilling. The pressure of the arms that enclosed her was slighter, less secure. The dark pools within the eyes, in the face that represented most of her contact with the world, shrank to pin-points, closing the connection that was her access to the only other life she could reach. She cried as little as possible. Things, she discovered, went more to her liking when she lay quietly and gurgled a little, and even better when she mimicked the long, horizontal shape the others made with their mouths. She found that by pulling on the muscles on the lower half of her face (her eyes were unaffected and remained watchful) she could get their eyes to widen with warmth, allowing her to slip inside and take the comfort of feeling she was somewhere she belonged. If she wasn't theirs, they weren't hers. When all was to their satisfaction they would lift her and hold her close, surrounding her with warmth, strength and safety. And all for the small price of learning to twitch a few muscles. The meaning behind the twitching of facial muscles takes much longer to learn, and, perhaps, for more people than most would imagine, is never learnt at all.

Ivy and Gerald were pleased with what they had made.

'She's lovely,' Gerald would say to his wife and anyone else who asked. 'Aren't you a lovely little girl?' he would croon at Frances, who offered her extended mouth in return for the soothing sound. If there was a pang of disappointment, it took only a moment for him to realise that it was better this way. A daughter was a completely new beginning. Ivy watched him doting on the new baby and felt satisfied. Little Frances, the good, pretty baby, was a safety net; the sound of a key turning in a lock. Ivy felt safer than ever.

In truth the actual business of having a baby, the uncomfortable, late pregnancy, the misery of labour, the nappy-changes and late-night feeds, had been a bit of a strain. The nanny remained a fantasy; there was no room for one in the two-roomed flat, and it was difficult, in any case, to justify the need to Gerald considering that she was not occupied with anything else during the day. Gerald said the money would be better saved for the purchase of a house, somewhere in the suburbs, perhaps. Though there was a note of . . . hesitancy? Or something, anyway, that she didn't care to examine too closely. But Ivy liked the idea of a suburban house to replace the city flat, and began designing it in her mind during the hours when Frances slept and there was nothing else to do.

But the pram was real enough. A monument to British craftsmanship was how they described it in the brochure. It was certainly impressive. The glassy black-lacquered coachwork with its sleek swirls of silver chrome decoration bounced gently on the big-wheeled silvered chassis. Frances was almost lost in its cavernous interior, a tiny face set on a broderie anglaise pillowcase, peering out above the matching eiderdown, and shaded from the world by an imposing black hood. She could see only her proud mother, but from time to time a face would appear around the edge of the hood, a stranger gazing in to see the contents of so fine a carriage and commenting favourably. London after the war retained the camaraderie of the blitz; people stopped to look at the new babies and expressed their approval of the new life being perambulated along the streets. Ivy loved to walk around

London with Frances in the pram and receive congratulations from the passers-by. She kept the hood up even when it wasn't raining because she found it increased people's curiosity and she was more often stopped and asked, 'Is that a baby you've got in there? Oh, let me see . . .' That kind of thing. And a cool finger would connect with the end of Frances's nose, or press down gently on her belly.

Ivy was more than happy to share the details of her daughter with these friendly strangers. Yes, she was a good baby, she slept all through the night, *and* much of the day. She enumerated the number of bottles Frances took, her satisfactory weight gain, her precise age in weeks and the fact that the father was, indeed, very proud of his little girl. Frances took the opportunity to exercise her facial muscles and gurgle, happy to discover that all the faces peering down at her delighted in her twitching muscles. She enjoyed these sudden adventures in sight and sound in what was otherwise the dark and uneventful, if pleasantly bouncy, experience of her daily outing.

– Do I detect a certain wistfulness in your description of your mother's babyhood?

– You do not. I can't be beguiled by half a story. Not when I know the other half. The warm glow of a family welcoming the new-born is only attractive if you don't know what happens next.

– My mistake. Perhaps I wanted to hear the note of warmth I only thought I heard for a second or two.

– If you wanted something life-affirming you should have had yourself invented by a narrator more capable of cerebral dreaming. Me, I'm just grateful I didn't begin on a wave of hope, only to find myself drowning before I reached the shore.

– Very poetic.

– You're getting a bit cocky for someone who could be snuffed out – just like that.

– Are you sure I'd be so easy to get rid of, now I'm here and listening?

– When my mother first held me in her arms, in the hospital, and the nurse had turned away to suppress the urge to put a pillow over my face, she whispered to me, 'I won't be able to do you any harm, little one. I can't damage you. That's my maternal gift to you.' If you're looking for sentiment from me, that would be where you'd find it. If it were there to find. What a gift! To be told at birth that nothing in my whole life would ever hurt me. What a mother! Being what I am, could I have asked for a better mother than the one I was born to?

– Isn't that tautologous? Anyway, how could you hear her?

– I've told you before, you're hidebound by logic. I *heard* her in my way.

43

– So, go on about your mother.

– Continue the story, you mean?

– Yes.

– Things go from bad to unrelenting from here.

– I can cope.

– Good. Actually, it's not all bad, not entirely dreary. There's some glory in it if you see it from the right angle.

– Your angle?

– Is there any other? Are you listening?

– I'm listening.

IT WOULDN'T HAVE surprised anyone but Ivy to learn that her feeling of safety was quite illusory. Gerald's vagueness about the suburban house was as telling as it seemed. But not to poor Ivy, wrapped in mink-lined, Big Ben doorchiming dreams. If she heard his hesitation, she didn't listen. How could she, stuck there in the Fifties' gloom, over forty, with a young child, without skills or resources, with nothing actually, except a notion of how things ought to be? Either she had what she thought she had, or she had nothing.

She had, of course, nothing. But nothing can get you quite a long way, for a while.

Once rationing was eased and the black market became no more than a recent memory, the flow of money to the Pepper household began to falter. Gerald tried to put his entrepreneurial talents to other uses, but nothing worked out well enough, for long enough. The quiet hum of conversation in the next room, that Frances had listened to as a baby, changed to the grating sound of disappointed adults bickering: a high-pitched wail of complaint, like the noise of a saw cutting through metal, told of Ivy's increasing anxiety and sense that things were not working out exactly as planned; a low, dull monotone from Gerald held the threat that his boredom and anger would not be kept in check indefinitely.

Money was the centre of the circle they were trapped inside. Ivy had no other way of taking her place in the world. She only had visible signs to reassure herself. The flat and Frances were the visible signs into which money had to be poured. For the flat it was necessary to have the very latest of everything. New furniture, fresh paint, different curtains proved that everything was all right. For Frances, appropriately dressed as the Princess who proved her mother a Queen, there had to be private dancing, skating, music lessons; a

45

good – as in fashionable and expensive – school; the manners and appearance of a lady. Frances and the flat had to have what was obviously the best of everything that money could buy.

Gerald knew, nervously, the condition of the bank account, and that Frances could not continue in her private school, and nor could the flat have the 'lick of paint' that Ivy insisted it needed. He reacted by staying as quiet as he could and looking with increasing desperation for a well-heeled exit. Ivy began to top up her dreams with gin again and the bills accrued in a haze of alcohol. Little Frances's dresses became frothier; the layers of stiff, scratchy net petticoats getting deeper as the demands for settlement grew more insistent. She had a pair of white gloves for every outfit.

'A lady,' Ivy would remind her eight year old, 'is never seen without a pair of gloves.' No one, at any rate, on the cover of *Vogue* or the *Ladies' Home Journal*, was to be seen without them.

Side by side with the gloves went Goodness. Apart from gloves, Frances was never to be seen without nice manners and a polite smile, especially, essentially, in public. Good girls went shopping without complaint and practised their *pliés* for their forthcoming career as prima ballerinas and from thence a more-than-good marriage. Good girls smiled shyly and said 'please' and 'thank you' invariably, and 'everything is fine' when asked. Good girls were a credit to their mothers, and, in return, their mothers assured them that life would be wonderful and could only get better and better.

But Frances was no fool. She didn't hear the sound of better and better in the duet of screech and mumble she listened to at night, when the darkness of her room was supposed to render her deaf.

She came to regard the white gloves and stiff petticoats as more than just uncomfortable. They, along with the *pliés* and arpeggios and shy smiles, became hateful indications of the lies she guessed she was being told. If many of her generation were brought up in a world where the grown-ups made things all right and safe, Frances, born into the same world, developed an early understanding that the grown-ups were dangerous liars to be trusted at one's peril. The promised security of tight arms around her in infancy had been deceptive. The knowledge that adults did not keep their promises gave her a certain edge over her contemporaries when it came to unpleasant surprises later on in life.

Frances was still very young when she made her first private communion with herself. She was still too young to declare the truth of what she had discovered, and too vulnerable and dependent to doubt openly the stories she was told.

One afternoon Frances stood in silence in front of the mirror in her bedroom. She was dressed and ready to go to a party, her own, with a magician and extravagant presents for the guests.

She wore a pure white party dress, made of fine net, with a tight bodice, short puffed sleeves, and a wide, pale pink cummerbund that tied in a big, floppy bow at the back. The skirt just skimmed her skinny knees and stuck out at a forty-five degree angle, like an abbreviated crinoline. On her feet she wore pink satin ballet slippers and short white ankle socks, their tops neatly turned down. Her thick, deep auburn hair was pulled back and tied, ballerina-style, into a bun at the nape of her neck with a satin bow, similar to the one around her waist, its pastel pinkness lost in the drama of her rag-ringleted red locks. Her hands were concealed by short white gloves with a tiny lace edging that finished at the prominent bones of her thin wrists.

Frances stared at herself in the mirror. She hated all of it: the dress, the shoes, the bow in her hair, the gloves. She hated the vulnerable look of her naked legs between the tops of her socks and the bottom edge of her dress. She hated the skinny arms that showed from wrist to elbow. She stood in front of the mirror and tried to make her face look as sour as she felt. She couldn't. Somehow the clothes enforced the polite smile she saw reflected back at her. Nothing she did would make it go away; the muscles seemed frozen. She glared at the pretty, smiling child in the mirror and hesitantly, carefully, for the very first time, said:

'Fuck.'

The initial articulation was tentative; a long 'f', the final 'k' sound a little soft, almost a question. 'Fuck?' But she heard that it was basically right, checking against the memory of the word she had heard in the night from the room next door. The word was right, but had to be sharper and shortened at either end to get that feeling she experienced when she heard it from the other room. She tried again, her sharp, bony face tense with concentration.

'Fuck.'

'Fuck.'

'Fuck.'

She didn't know what it meant, didn't think it meant anything, but she understood what it did. A bad word, never said in front of her, a short explosion that happened only at night. She remembered the variations.

'Fuck . . . fuck-ing. Fucking. Fucking.'

She had it now.

'Fucking dress. Fucking socks. Fucking gloves. Fucking *liars!*' she told herself in the mirror in the tones of a nicely brought-up little girl. 'Fucking liars. Fuck. Fuck. Fuck.'

It was a magic word. As she spoke it the white dress became spattered with mud, her gloves lost and the shops suddenly out of stock of replacements. 'I'm sorry, Madam, but we've had a particular run on white gloves. We can't get them for love nor money.' Her red hair hung loose and unbrushed, a wild tangle around her face. And her face . . . the smile had disappeared. There, in the mirror, was a wicked, scowling face, cross; a credit to no one. Here was a shocking little girl with a face to match, who lived in a deep, secret place that could only be reached by the power of the Word. A strong, magnificent, dreadfully dreadful, filthy little girl. The triumph bloomed and burst inside her. It was her moment. Frances's moment. If she could have, she would have taken her reflection in her arms and whirled them both around the room with the pure joy and energy of that moment. Badness raged beneath the lace, and she had found it: vivid and alive and herself.

– That's glory, all right.

– I told you, didn't I? It's so glorious I'd get up and do a small dance myself, if I could.

– But you can't.

– No. I'll never be wicked. Nor good, nor selfish, nor generous.

– It's a pity.

– It isn't anything, it's just a fact.

– You enjoy it, though?

– What?

– The passion your mother had at that moment.

– Yes, she had energy . . . passion, whatever you care to call it. It was there in its way. Shall I go on?

– Please. I'm listening.

'WHAT DID YOU say?' Ivy asked vaguely, as she entered the room where Frances was practising her first obscenity.

Frances blinked at Ivy through the mirror.

'Nothing. I was just rehearsing my "thank you's".' The scowl had vanished and the smile returned. The mud disappeared from the pretty white dress. But it didn't matter; she knew, now, how to get them back again.

So Frances discovered a deep pool of wickedness inside herself and dived into it when necessary like a fisher for pearls. It wouldn't make her life easier, but difficulty wasn't what she was trying to escape from.

Badness became Frances's secret. For safety and disguise she continued to be the outwardly good girl she had been taught to be. But for each virtuous act she performed the bad girl deep inside her lit a dark candle, until a strange illumination glowed in the place that now came to seem the real centre of herself. She thought of it as 'Badness' because there was no other way that she could see of distinguishing the black energy from the stuff she knew was called 'Good'. Names mattered. Things had to have names.

Frances continued to smile and say she liked things when she didn't. She pretended not to notice that Ivy was more frequently drunk, that Gerald was more often absent, and that even when he was present in the flat he was hardly there either for Ivy or herself. She continued to appear deaf to the sound of the dialogue from the next room although, in fact, it grew louder and more desperate.

But now all her virtues and pretences were accompanied by bolts of rage which accumulated through the day. At night she discharged the fury. Lying in bed and taking advantage of the noise coming from the next room, she would whisper the truth into the darkness.

'I hate school. I hate my friends. I hate saying thank you. I hate Daddy. I hate Mummy. And I wish she was dead. And I wish he was dead. I wish they were all dead. I wish everybody was dead. Fuck them. I wish, I wish, I wish . . . Amen.'

She whispered each word with a clear and precise articulation as if she were dictating a telegram that had to be understood and transcribed perfectly. The words were treasures from her underground storehouse of power, that could be examined only in secret. Every word had on each occasion to be poured over and appreciated to the full. She savoured the short syllables of *hate* and *dead* and capped their excitement with the dangerous thrill of her wishes. It was a form of prayer, potent and satisfying. When she was finished, and had whispered 'Amen' with special intensity, she waited in a sweat of terror for her prayer to be answered.

Each time she expected silence to fall in the next room. She saw herself creeping out of the bedroom to find her parents in the living-room struck down with the power of her words. She saw her mother slumped back over a chair, her dead eyes staring, her mouth open, liquid spilling from the glass still clutched in her outflung arm, caught in full flood by the lightning strike of her daughter's supplications. She saw her father face down on the floor by the door, stopped, dead in his tracks, as he made to slam out of the flat. But each night the sound continued: the shouting, the door slamming, the sound of glass and bottles clinking, and her mother's final drunken monologue of abuse that brought the night's events to an end. Every night she fell asleep, reprieved and disappointed. Every morning she woke to hear Ivy groaning about her headache, and was filled with guilt, grateful that her mother was still alive, but hopeful for the coming night.

Frances had a new problem at this point in her life. There was a split between the meanings of the words she used to describe herself and the way the world used them. And this confused her. She understood that the world, her mother, would have described her as good on the outside and bad on the inside, but there was no question that she *felt* good on the inside and bad on the outside. She experienced herself, in her deepest and most private place, as both wicked and entirely free of sin. She was both innocent and damned, equally, and each for precisely the same reasons.

Naturally the strain began to show. She developed a nervous tic. A tension vibrated the top of her spine, and ran up through her long neck to her cranium. It could only be discharged by a high arching, stretching movement of her neck, backwards, upwards and then down, so that her head made a forward circle in the air; a strange, almost elegant, birdlike movement, but disturbing because it was purposeless. Ivy told her to stop it when she noticed.

'It's not nice.'

'What?'

'Stop doing that. It's not nice. What will people think?'

But the tic became more frequent, until Frances found herself having to perform the movement every few minutes. Her schoolmates noticed too, and began to mimic her. They called her 'Duckling'.

'Duckling diving for fish?' they would chant at her in the playground. But Frances turned her head and lifted her shoulders as she walked away from them.

Eventually, irritated and embarrassed by the strange behaviour of her otherwise good little girl, Ivy took her to the doctor. Frances sat with her gloved hands folded in her lap, and her ankles neatly crossed six inches from the floor and smiled politely at the doctor. He asked her if everything was all right, was she worried about anything, at school, at home, perhaps? Frances smiled and shook her head.

'No,' she said, 'thank you, everything's fine. Nothing's wrong.'

Ivy confirmed this.

'Everything's fine, Doctor. Nothing's wrong.'

The doctor gave Ivy a prescription for Frances.

'A bottle of tonic,' he said, reassuringly. 'She's probably a bit run-down. Nothing to worry about. Just part of growing up. Just a stage.'

Frances added the doctor to the list of her night-time prayer.

It was a stage, and it did pass. The childish belief in the elemental power of her wishes couldn't be sustained for very long. The guilt and fear, which were bad enough, were joined by frustration. Whatever dark god she prayed to began to look ineffectual. The power, she came to understand, was not in her wishes, but in her wickedness. Being secretly wicked was all very well. It was like having a perfect singing voice but never uttering a note. What was the point?

Frances began to conceive of wickedness for herself as a career, as other little girls decided to be vets, or air hostesses, or married happily ever after. At that stage it was no more than a generalised notion, she had no specific activities in mind. She didn't really know what was available in the field, being too young and genuinely innocent of the world. She knew with a growing certainty that the secret shocking girl who lived behind the door that she had opened when she said 'fuck' for the first time would eventually leave her underground room and come out to accompany her into the real world. She felt confident that *she* would know what to do when the time came.

Frances's new dedication to wickedness did not prevent life around her from falling further into disarray, but it did give her a private place to go when things outside got tough. The subterranean cavern she found inside herself remained lit, although sometimes it seemed to have shrunk so that there was little more than a candle's worth of room for her to squeeze herself into. When that happened she had to work hard to get there, but she found a way to expand the diminished space inside herself with her breathing, pushing aside the dark, enclosing walls and making room. Then the other candles would flame to life and their curious light made her special place seem larger than the world itself. It was like one of those party tricks, where a magician pulls from a cylinder impossible lengths of coloured material, then a bunch of bright paper flowers and finally a rabbit. Far more than the visible exterior could possibly contain. Frances wasn't fooled by those tricks. She didn't know how they worked, but she knew they were mere tricks. And that was what mattered. But Frances's inner space, the glorious, bad, bright place, was unfathomable. She couldn't work it out at all, and had to come to the conclusion that some things in life had to be accepted with all their mystery intact.

It's my own place, she thought, and felt the warmth circulate around her body as it had when she was a baby and the deceitful adult arms enclosed her.

Ivy and Gerald noticed that all the fun had gone out of life, but they couldn't work out why either. They argued about money; her spending it, him not making enough of it. They argued about his late nights out and his distance from his wife and child. Occasionally, they settled for silence, and stopped speaking to each other except for the odd grunt over the dinner table.

There were times when all was well, almost as it had been during the war, before Frances was born. But those times became fewer as the years passed. There were nights when the conversation from the other room changed to giggles and whispers, and for the following day or two a rosy haze settled on the three of them in the small flat. Ivy left the bottle of gin in the sideboard, or shared a social drink before she presented Gerald with especially nice dinners. They would talk about the headlines in the evening paper; even, sometimes, ask the woman upstairs to stay with Frances while they went out to the cinema. On Saturdays they might, all three of them, go out for lunch and take Frances to a film. A threesome. A happy family.

Strangely, these times became the worst of all for Frances. They didn't last. Ivy would find something in Gerald's pocket, or he would be home late. Someone, any of them, would say something wrong. And the old days would return. Normality would return. The good days, scattered about, shafts of light in the overall shadow, were anguish for Frances, loving them and hating them because she knew they would end. Every moment she wondered when this good time would finish. By the time she was six she had no problem about the background colour of the zebra. It was black, with white stripes.

Now and then Gerald was rescued. Women whom Ivy referred to as 'that floozy' provided an occasional retreat, and Gerald took his leave of Ivy and Frances, telling himself that everyone makes a mistake or two in life, and that he owed it to himself to give himself one last chance. But he always came back. Things never worked out with the floozy and it wasn't only women who didn't have anywhere else to go.

Ivy drank and spent a lot of time staring at the wall of the living-room telling Frances, if she were there to listen, of her thwarted hopes.

'This isn't how it was going to be. Not how it was supposed to be. In the old days . . . in the old days . . . during the war, I had a dress of oyster satin with a little train that dragged along the ground. It was off-the-shoulder and I wore a tiny bunch of violets, just here.' She pressed a finger into her shoulder. 'On my naked skin. It was so . . . original. Everyone said so. How original it was. There were parties. We had card parties here, and in the middle the air-raid siren would go off, but we wouldn't take any notice. If our number's on it, we said . . . and then later, when everyone had gone home . . . do you know, one night I lost five hundred pounds at chemmy, but it didn't matter . . . when they'd all gone and we were alone with the cards all over the table, empty glasses everywhere, your father . . . he couldn't get enough of me in those days, when the war was on. He said there wasn't a corner of the flat where we hadn't . . . and there wasn't. Sometimes he wouldn't let me wipe the stains off the carpet . . . afterwards, when we'd finished. He said he wanted to be reminded whenever he looked at it. Look at the bloody carpet – filthy, threadbare thing. We need a new one. They don't last for ever, but, oh no, we can't afford it, he says. What does he care, he's never here to notice that it's wearing out . . .'

Usually her speech was so slurred that it was hard to

understand the words. But Frances didn't listen, anyway. She spent most of her time in her secret sanctuary.

The only thing that went on as normal were the outward signs of Frances's goodness. The white gloves, the ankle socks, and the polite smiles were more necessary than ever to Ivy.

Gerald and Ivy maintained their drab and unhappy marriage, each with fading memories of what it was they had hoped for to start with, each knowing that they had used up all their chances. Well, they were desperate and disappointing times. Lots of people sank in the disillusioning mudflats of the Fifties. War isn't good for people's sense of reality and, when the excitement of strange times is over, the world looks dreadfully dingy, all the glitter and promise replaced by brickdust and bombsites.

The block of bombed, derelict houses across the road from the flat had been a near miss for Ivy and Gerald, one night in the good old days of the blitz. The adrenalin had raced; they really knew they were alive, and had celebrated with a feast of copulation. But for Frances, twelve years later, it became the nursery where she took her first steps on the path that until now had been no more than a sketchily drawn map lying in a drawer in the back of her mind.

Several adjoining houses had been demolished in the raid. Now it was a bizarre landscape of grey brick and rubble grown over with groundsel, shepherd's purse, dandelions and nettles. Here and there a wall had stayed standing, the pattern of the rooms still visible as squares of ghostly floral wallpaper. A firegrate remained in place on what must once have been an upstairs bedroom, a shattered sink still clung to the remains of a kitchen wall, a torn, filthy curtain fluttered through a broken window. It had the air of a shocking revelation, of privacy ripped away. Here were Mr and Mrs Jones's domestic arrangements laid bare for all the world to see, with everything that had made it comfortable, their *home*, blown away by wind and war and time. What was left seemed like nature's sneering comment on the temporality and pettiness of human organization. The acre of bombsite was the world how it would be when all the people had gone. Rubble and weeds and crumbling monuments to family life.

Frances loved it.

Although she had passed it every day to and from school, she had never been on to the site. Ivy had told her not to, it was dirty and dangerous. The newspapers were full of stories of children who had died when a wall had toppled, or the shiny something they found had exploded as they touched it.

Frances walked past the bombsite in her white gloves and shined shoes and found its dangerous, wild landscape a perfect match for her internal topography. She knew it was her place, but hesitated, every afternoon, never quite able to make the decision to leave the well-made pavement that was her route home. There was a finality about taking the step across the boundary of close-fitting concrete to the waiting wilderness. There would be a moment when she hovered, with a foot in both worlds, when something would be lost and something gained, and a change would occur that made a difference. But that thought itself, full though it was with nameless dangers, was enough to make the step inevitable. The danger, itself, pushed her towards action. Frances was never able not to do something once she had acknowledged it was there to do.

She took the step, without having planned to, on a day that was no different from any other. Ivy, at home nursing her disappointments, would be satisfied with a story of a last-minute errand for her teacher and late buses. Frances stepped carefully off the edge of the pavement and went on to the site. She made her way to the other side of a crumbling but still-upright wall that stood alone, two storeys high, and concealed her from the passers-by in the street. She bent down and undid the buckles of her shoes, slipped them off and placed them side by side on top of her satchel, behind a pile of bricks. She peeled off her socks and put one in each shoe. Then she unzipped her skirt, undid the buttons of her blouse and cardigan and undressed, folding the clothes neatly into a pile on top of her shoes. She stood for a moment in her white vest and knickers and looked around. Old bricks, broken and crumbling, covered the ground in heaps like

57

rolling sand dunes in a desert of rubble. And, like a desert, patches of tough vegetation designed to thrive in a hostile environment flourished and grew with a triumphant vigour, breaking through the brickdust and piles of broken remains of buildings.

Frances clambered towards the centre of the site, stumbling over the mounds of rubble, stinging and scraping her bare legs on the nettles and sharp edges of brick and stone. She was heading for an empty space she had seen, a bald circle of scrappy grass and weeds. Frances spent the next hour collecting all the unbroken bricks she could find in the surrounding area and with them built a low wall, two bricks high, around the empty patch of ground, enclosing it. When she had finished she arranged a rectangle of four bricks in the middle of the space and sat down on them, ankles crossed, chin cradled in her hands, in the centre of the home she had built for the bad girl to live in.

Ivy accepted her story about the errand but was furious about the fall she had had in the playground.

'Look at your legs, all grazed and scratched like a street urchin. Haven't you got any sense? You don't have to run around like a wild thing in the playground. Why can't you play nice, quiet games? It's lucky you didn't ruin your skirt. What will your dance teacher say when she sees what your legs look like?'

Frances apologized.

'I've been invited to Susan's home for tea tomorrow. Her mother will pick us both up.'

'What does he do, her father?'

Frances shrugged.

'I think he's in business of some kind,' Ivy murmured to herself. 'I've seen *her* at the school. She's a very well-groomed woman. Yes, that's all right, but make sure you behave properly. Remember to say thank you for everything and speak nicely.'

The next day Frances waited anxiously for school to end, terrified that her wall would be gone when she arrived. But it was there, exactly as she had left it.

She spent whatever time she could at her secret place over

the next few days, sitting on her rectangle of bricks in the middle of the circle. At first she thought about making a table, and collecting some of the old bits of equipment that lay scattered over the site. There was a scarred enamel jug, and various dented, rusting kettles that would have made the beginnings of a kitchen. But she didn't. She kept the place empty and each afternoon she folded her clothes on top of her satchel, and scrambled over the debris to her wall where she sat for a little while, on her makeshift chair in her vest and knickers, reading a book she had brought with her. There wasn't anything else she particularly wanted to do.

The boy was a couple of years older than Frances, perhaps twelve, and he stood kicking up dust in the middle of her space. Frances lost her footing when she saw him and several bricks tumbled down the mound she stood on. The boy looked round and stared at her.

'You got no clothes on.'

'I have. I've got my vest and knickers on. Go away.'

'Why should I? You don't own this place.'

'I do. I made it. It's private, go away.'

'I won't.'

The boy walked to the edge of the circle and kicked a few bricks out of the wall.

'Stop it. Go away.'

Frances ran to the breach in the wall and began to repair it.

'It's stupid.'

'You're stupid.' Frances turned and shouted. 'It's my place. I found it. I built the wall.'

She ran at him, pushing him back from the wall with her head and hands against his chest.

'Go away! Go away!'

She was crying now, and heaving the boy back with all her strength to the perimeter of the wall. He stumbled as his heels came in contact with the bricks.

'Stupid girls. Fucking stupid girls.' He staggered over the wall to keep himself upright, then turned to kick a brick out of place before walking off a few yards. He squatted down on a pile of weed-covered bricks and began to investigate their undersides, ignoring Frances who had taken her place on her chair.

For a while there was silence. The boy examined his bricks, and Frances sat inside her wall scratching patterns on the dusty soil with a twig. She had noticed the ease with which the boy had used her magic word, as if he owned it. She wondered what he knew about being bad, but she went on pretending he wasn't there.

'You got red hair.'

Frances didn't look up.

'So what?'

The boy shrugged and silence broke out again as they both got on with their activities. After a little while the boy stood up, straddling the piles of bricks like a mountaineer.

'If you take your knickers off, I'll show you my cock.'

Frances had found her first opportunity for wickedness.

She examined it carefully. No question that what lurked beneath her knickers was private; more than private – secret, dangerous, bad. Something had happened behind the boiler-house in the playground that had caused parents to come up to school and several boys and a girl from the top class to be absent for half a term. The point was no one spoke about it, in the same way that her parents didn't speak about her 'private parts', as Ivy called it. It didn't have a name, it didn't even seem to be a unity. The quality of unspeakableness was the same at school and at home; a low murmuring, a whisper that ceased as soon as she came near. Frances had been intrigued but remained substantially ignorant. The boy's offer had all the intonation of the gossip about the boiler-house, but this time it was said aloud and at least *something* had been named.

'I don't want to see your cock,' Francis said, meaning more that she wasn't completely sure she knew what it was.

'Yes, you do,' the boy told her, still astride his pile of bricks. 'It's interesting. And I'll help you build your wall higher if you do.' He sounded more friendly now.

'All right,' Frances said and began to slide her knickers towards her feet, 'but not for long.'

Given her vague but definite expectations, Frances was surprised to find herself unmoved by what she saw when the boy unzipped his trousers. She was even a little disappointed that wickedness should be so small, pink and inoffensive. It didn't compare at all with her brightly-lit inner temple. It took a long moment before she understood why there had been all the whispers and silence about the boiler-house incident. At first she thought she must have misunderstood and felt that she would *never* find the actions that matched her gnawing hunger to be bad.

But she had been looking in the wrong direction.

When she raised her eyes to look at the boy's face, she saw that she was on the right track after all. He was still staring down, as she had been a moment before, so that, then, the trajectories of their eyes had crossed. Now her shifted gaze made up an angle of desire: her eyes to his eyes; his eyes to her private part. It was the expression in his eyes, not the sight of what lay beneath his trousers, that explained the mystery to Frances.

Sinfulness shone out of the boy's eyes; the greed and hunger glowing from them, just at the sight of what she carried about with her all the time; of what was, for her, no more than part of her – arm, leg, private part. Except that sleeves could be dispensed with when the weather was warm, and shorts worn on sunny days, but knickers were mandatory, whatever the condition. Her thrill was not from his uncovered genitals, but the excitement that her own engendered in him. Desire, she discovered, was about being desired. But for the bold, bad boy, whose name turned out to be Stuart, desire was focused on the object.

It was a crucial lesson for Frances to learn at so tender an age. It gave her what she most needed at the time – a sense, at least for the time being, of direction.

'Well, are you going to stand there all day, staring?' Frances demanded, crossing her arms over her flat chest. The boy looked up at her, surprised, it seemed, that she could talk and move.

'Well,' Frances insisted, 'what do we do now?'

The truth was that neither of them was sure *what* was to be done next. This was still the Fifties. What they knew about sexual behaviour was minimal, and Nature, although it had done well in recolonizing the bomb-torn cityscape, did not live up to its reputation for ensuring that everyone knows what to do when the time comes. But they had learned enough about the world to know that she should ask and he should come up with a suggestion. It was clear that the boy felt it reasonable that he should be expected to make the next move, but equally clear that he could do no more than stand there with his trousers round his knees and stare.

'What's it doing?' Frances nodded her head at his penis. 'It's getting bigger.'

The boy looked down at himself.

'That's what it does,' he mumbled.

'Is that all? Aren't we supposed to *do* anything?'

'I sort of rub it until I've finished.'

'How do you know you've finished?'

'This stuff comes out and I feel better.'

'Stuff?' Frances began to feel slightly alarmed.

'It's called spunk. It's wet.'

'Like weeing?'

The boy shrugged.

'Well, come over here and show me.'

The boy shuffled knock-kneed across the rubble holding his trousers with one hand, and crossed the wall into Frances's space. He let the trousers fall around his ankles and, after a momentary hesitation, clamped his palm around his penis, and began to pump frantically. Frances watched in silence for a moment. The boy's breathing quickened and his eyes locked on to the small, naked mound between her legs.

'Can I have a go?'

Frances reached out to take over.

'Is it all right if I do it slower?'

The boy blinked up at her, and nodded in time to the

movements of Frances's hand, which was now working at half the speed of his own efforts.

'What if I hold it tighter?' she asked, tightening her grip. 'Or looser?'

Now she barely brushed it with her palm. The boy made a sound like someone with a bad stomach ache.

'Are you all right?'

'Go on,' the boy panted. 'Do it fast now . . . go on . . .'

Frances learned a lot that afternoon, more than she could yet put a name to. Nature is greatly aided by human curiosity. The desire to find out, to experiment, has always been a boon to the human race. Curiosity was Frances's instinctive reaction to her first sexual encounter. What happens if . . . ? Isn't it interesting that . . . ? It was very interesting how the brick-kicking bully had become this gasping, needing boy who seemed to be in pain but didn't mind. More interesting still was the fact that nothing more than taking down her knickers had effected the transformation.

Now, though, the boy's eyes were closed and his breathing came in short, heavy gasps. Her naked lower half was no longer the point.

It *was* like weeing, but stickier, Frances thought, as she looked around for something to wipe her hand on. Stuart sniffed a couple of times and pulled up his trousers before squatting down on the ground. Frances wiped her hand on her knickers as she pulled them up and sat on her brick chair. Stuart picked up the twig she had been using and scraped at the ground.

'Do you want to do it again?' Frances asked.

'No. Tomorrow.'

'All right. Do you want to do the wall now?'

They worked methodically, at opposite sides of the circle, collecting bricks and building a third level on to the existing wall.

Frances spent that evening and night, before going to sleep, thinking about the boy on the bombsite. The sound of Ivy and Gerald bickering in the next room faded to a background hum as she congratulated herself on her amazingly good luck in finding just what she was looking for. In particular, she remembered his eyes as he looked at her. She took the experience, cupped carefully in the curved palms of her hands, down to her special place, ablaze that night with light. She stood in the centre of the circle of flaring candles and examined the events of the afternoon. The look on his face, the sensation that had given her, his speechless response to her varying touch, the hurried, hasty zipping-up of his trousers. Frances had made an excellent beginning, as wicked and exciting and mysterious as the girl in the mud-spattered dress who learned to say 'fuck' and taught herself to scowl could have hoped for.

−Aah, sex and power.

— As you say — Aah. Here we are at last. Of course, it doesn't do a thing for me.

— Nothing?

— I've got the equipment but none of the drive.

— Anyway, you'd be a bit young to appreciate it.

— I confess it baffles me, the inordinate attention the human race, with its remarkable expanse of temporal and parietal lobes, gives to sex.

— Perhaps you ought to make more effort to understand.

— Why? It's not my problem.

— But if you're telling the story of your mother. Sex seems to be becoming important to her.

— That's a very superficial view. It was the power of desire that my mother discovered on the bombsite. Not her desire, but the desire of the boy for her.

— But there was desire for power.

— Well, it's all a mystery to me. All right, let's try and make sense of it. Let's sit behind the boiler-house of my empty cranium and see what happens. Words seem to be all that's needed to start with. 'Tits,' you begin with a giggle. 'Cock!' I say and snigger. 'Willy!' you respond with a guffaw. I take a really deep breath. 'Cunt!' And we fall sideways, weak with the howls of laughter that completely overcome us. We laugh so much we can barely breathe as we gasp out the monosyllables. 'Balls!' 'Fuck!' 'Suck!' 'Clit!' By now our screams of hilarity have created a tidal wave of the liquid inside my skull, the reverberations whipping up a storm in the water where my brain would have been. It crashes against the sides of my head and we're carried from side to side by the great waves beating and beating against the prison of my skull until at last their power overwhelms the skin and bone, and breaks through, throwing us both out of our tiny universe into the reality outside, where we expire gasping like dying fish in the world we don't belong in.

— That sounds like one of your mother's stories.

— It is. I paraphrased. But it doesn't work, does it? The words don't have the power on their own. They're just words. Tell you what, I'll give you a long hard look at my cunt. Let's add organs to the words. Here it is: damp, fleshy folds. Moist, dark crevices. Mushroom country. Pastel pink against rough, dark red and, if I could get older, coarse curls spreading mystery over the shocking, private involutions. Nothing much, really. Not if you didn't know what it was and how private it had to be. Just skin folded and refolded, and empty space. It reminds me of me. Labia, lips, a smooth valley, inner lips, wrinkled and involuted, the labyrinthine entrance that I'll part for you to show what you've always longed to get a good long look at. Just a small hole, an opening, the mouth of my secret cave. Look as long and hard and carefully as you like. So that's what all the fuss is about. Well, well, well.

— I'm just here to listen.

— Well, the mystery remains unsolved. As Mother said, I don't have the brainpower to appreciate sex. It doesn't matter, I'm just telling the story. I don't have to understand it as well.

— But your mother did understand about sex.

— I told you, it wasn't sex. She understood about secrecy. It wasn't her fault that the most secret activity she could find was jiggling that boy's penis about. You don't seem to be listening as carefully as someone who has no other function than to listen ought.

— I'm all ears, I promise you.

— Shall I continue?

— I wish you would.

— I could just sink into oblivion for the rest of my short life. I don't have to do this, you know.

— I know. Still, it passes the time. And what else could I occupy myself with?

– For your sake then.
– For my sake, then, please go on.

FRANCES ENJOYED RECALLING and examining the small wave that had rippled through her as she watched Stuart's eyes sucking the sight of her into his brain. It was excitement, but mostly it was power – a sense of being able to pluck the strings of the world and listen, at leisure, to the reverberating sound she had created. And it was private, all hers, and the more powerful for keeping it to herself. She had something, she knew something, and the world, at best, could only guess how things were with her.

Frances and Stuart met regularly at the bombsite. The wall grew to five bricks high, but that was as far as they could go without mortar and skill. Instead of building higher, Frances suggested they make interior walls, carving up the space into two segments with a corridor running between.

'What about furniture?' Stuart suggested. 'We could build tables and things.'

Frances vetoed this.

'No,' she said firmly, 'this isn't a house, it's a place.'

The boy shrugged, a little disappointed. He liked making models.

When the inside walls were made, Frances insisted that they begin each session in separate rooms. She arrived and stood, in her vest and knickers, in one space; he had to wait in the other until she had taken off her knickers and called him. He could see her, of course, because the territory was only marked out with two rows of brick, but he wasn't to cross the corridor into her section until she called.

Frances, with her innate understanding of desire, took things slowly. It was several days before she said to him, as she stroked and squeezed, 'You can touch me, if you like.'

Stuart's uncertain, grubby finger edged nervously towards the small, dark space between Frances's legs.

She could hear Ivy saying, 'Never let anyone touch you . . . *there*. Do you understand? And don't touch yourself . . . *there* . . . either.'

And in answer to her inevitable question. 'Because it's dirty!' Ivy's face emphatic with disgust. 'It's not nice!'

In fact, it tickled more than anything, at least until she remembered Ivy's words and tone of voice, and saw Stuart's eyes, mere slits of concentration. Then there was something else, but indefinable.

'Go on, put your finger right into the hole.' Frances closed her hand tighter around Stuart's penis. She could see a pulse beating in his temple.

'Is that all right?' Stuart asked after a tentative penetration.

'Yes, it's quite nice. Make it go in further.'

Stuart wasn't sure if he wanted to put his finger in any deeper. His head was suddenly full of pictures of mousetraps, and car doors slamming shut. But he also wanted to know what was up there before he risked doing what all his friends claimed they had already done. 'Oh yeah, it's really great.' 'Well, it's, you know, sort of, fantastic . . . you *know*.' But he didn't, and there was something unconvincing, and certainly uninformative, about his friends' descriptions of the real thing.

He took the plunge and Frances closed her eyes tightly for a moment.

It was, really, nothing special for either of them, except that for the boy it was the first time he had explored the inside of another human being and, for her, the first time explored. The indefinable feeling that Frances had had remained undefined but grew strong with promise as Stuart ejaculated into her hand.

'You won't tell?' Stuart asked after that first digital penetration.

'Course I won't,' Frances said.

Nothing could have been further from her mind. Telling would have spoiled everything. The best time of all was when she sat at the dinner table with her sulking mother and morose father and overcame their silence with her own. She had, at last, something not to tell, that belonged to the real world. Her deadly night-time prayers, her candle-lit cavern were real enough to her, but she knew they wouldn't be substantial enough for the grown-up world. They wouldn't be taken seriously if she did tell, so her silence on the subject had less power and was as much for self-protection as anything. If she spoke of her wicked self in terms she understood, they would have given her another bottle of tonic.

Her meetings with Stuart were different, even if, to her, they stemmed from the same, more important source. Of course she wouldn't tell. The bombsite, the folding of her outer clothing, what she and Stuart did, his eyes when he looked at her; these were treasures to be kept secure. Not the acts themselves, of course, but the power of not telling anyone about them. Stuart was perfectly safe.

But Frances didn't feel very safe. As she had grown older, six, eight, ten now, she began to see Ivy and Gerald more clearly as people who were inadequate to the task of living. They seemed, increasingly, like children playing house without any adult to sort out the squabbles and mess. All the rules were being broken, and all their energy was taken up with complaint, and accusation of the other for not playing properly. It was no different, so far as Frances could see, from the games she watched being played at school. Except that this was supposed to be real life and nobody ever seemed to come along and sort anything out. The game itself had been lost, and had become entirely centred on how it should be played. Points, these days, were only granted for spotting contraventions of the rules. Frances lived with a sense of imminent danger.

The louder and more continual the shouting and the door slamming got, the more she withdrew, as, in the first tremors of an earthquake, knowing that nowhere was safe, one might hold very still, as if stillness itself would provide protection from the falling masonry and the gaping chasms in the earth. Frances held still, squatting in her secret place, her illuminated temple, and considered her position. In there she was the strong, bad girl who spoke words of power and did wicked things with the boy on the bombsite. Outside, in the other world, she was supposed to be good; a smiling, pretty child, immobilised by propriety. Somewhere in the middle was a terror that it wasn't useful to examine. Her real life was held together by very little. Perhaps by no more than a pair of white gloves.

Frances met Stuart at the bombsite every evening after tea and, sometimes, if she could slip out of the playground without being seen, during lunch-break too.

She looked forward to these encounters only partly for the pleasure of what she saw in Stuart's eyes, her power over his desire. The real pleasure, the main point of the exercise, was in providing herself with something to be quiet about.

'Were you good at school today?' Ivy asked when Frances got home.

'Yes.' Smiling, taking off her gloves and coat.

'That's my good girl. You'll have to have bread and something for tea, I didn't manage to get to the shops today. I don't know where the day went . . .'

Frances cut herself some of yesterday's loaf and spread it with whatever she could find in the cupboard. As she was eating she thought about how she had met Stuart at the bombsite that lunch-break, and about getting out after tea to meet him again. She didn't mull over the details of what she'd done or would do, it was the thinking itself that mattered. When Ivy was in the room she thought at the top of her voice. She thought so loud and hard it seemed impossible that Ivy couldn't hear. But still she didn't.

Anyway, Ivy had thoughts of her own. She wondered when Gerald would be home. Then she wondered if Gerald would be home. In the early days she had only wondered the former, then, as things began to go wrong, she began to wonder the latter. Now she wondered both, but not because she missed him. She wished she knew if and when Gerald would be back because she wanted to know how long she had to get good and drunk so he could see how he had ruined her life.

'I'll show *him*,' she muttered with a vicious twist of the

gin-bottle top. She drank through most of the day now, so that being out and out drunk was something of a special effort.

When that drink was finished she poured another, and sat down beside Frances at the table. The smell of Ivy's face powder wafted across the table, pink, sweet and heavy. Sometimes, when she sat down or moved too suddenly, small clouds of dust drifted down from her cheeks like an advance warning of an avalanche. Ivy made up heavily and clumsily these days; the rouge too red and badly blended, the lipstick thick and bright. Frances sometimes feared that Ivy wasn't there at all any more, only the grey roots creeping up the excessively black hair gave her some reassurance.

'Your father never came in last night. Off with some floozy. While I sit here all night worrying about the bills. You need new shoes, you've gone and scuffed those. You can't walk around looking like that. Try telling him that, he doesn't care. He doesn't care about anything but his women. Why can't you be more careful? What do you think people will think if they see you walking around with shoes like that? They'll think . . .'

It was too awful to contemplate what they might think.

I wonder, Frances thought at full volume, what they would think if they saw me holding Stuart's willy in my hand and heard the funny sound he makes when he comes. She smiled a little to herself.

'Do you think it's funny? Do you think it's a joke?' Ivy screamed, banging her glass on the table, making Frances jump at the noise.

'No.'

I took my knickers down at lunch-time and let Stuart put his finger up . . . there. Do you think that's funny?

'Can I go out after tea and play with Susan?' Frances asked aloud.

'You're spending a lot of time with that Susan. Well, make sure you don't get dirty, and don't go near the bombsite, and be back in time to wash your hair. I don't want to sit around waiting for you as well as him. Understand?'

'Yes, Mummy.' The good girl smiled and washed her plate at the sink.

'There's a good girl.' Ivy mellowed as she poured herself another drink. 'You're all I've got in the world. The only thing I have to show for . . .'

Ivy still couldn't understand how things had happened the way they had, but she was beginning to understand that they wouldn't ever get any better. So she searched in an alcohol-driven meditation, hour upon hour, for *what had gone wrong*. She could make no sense of any of it. The contradiction of the memory of fun and happiness and prospects with the way things were now was an impossible knot to unravel. Nothing had happened and yet this was how it was. Of course the war was over, and the money wasn't there any more, and Gerald wouldn't take an interest in anything but his floozies. But . . . why? How could there have been so much . . . gaiety . . . and now this . . . nothing . . . this getting older and no one caring and no more . . . fun? Her eyes were glassy now with tears that would begin to spill any moment. But Frances had already left the house, and Ivy wept alone, the tears coursing down her cheeks, making muddy tracks as the salt water mixed with Helena Rubinstein's La Rochelle face powder.

Poor Ivy. The truth was nobody did care much about her. It wasn't her fault, but there wasn't much to care about. She never could see that, if you allow yourself to be blown about by the wind for too long, there comes a point when there's no substance left at all. There's nothing left to retrieve even if the wind drops. It was a piece of information someone should have given her long before. But no one did.

'You're late,' Ivy mumbled as Gerald slammed the front door behind him at ten o'clock that night.

'Meeting,' he said, pulling at his collar and tie. 'Drunk again, I see.' He sat down with his back to her in an armchair with the evening paper.

'What else is there for me to do? Whose fault is it?' her voice rising dangerously.

'Yours,' Gerald said in a bored monotone.

'I'll leave you.'

Gerald didn't answer beyond a slight lifting of his eyes to the heavens. Ivy couldn't see, but she didn't have to.

'I'll kill myself. I'll take an overdose.'

Gerald didn't look up from his paper.

'Take some for me, while you're at it.'

Ivy cleared the table with the back of her forearm. The glass, bottles, ashtray, crashed to the floor. Gerald turned the page.

'You bastard, you don't care. This isn't a life. This is hell.'

Gerald nodded agreement as Ivy ran into the kitchen. She came out wielding a vegetable knife and made for Gerald.

'I'll kill you,' she screamed, waving the knife wildly. 'You deserve to die. We'll all die. I'll do her in and then myself. I'll kill us all. There's nothing for any of us to be alive for.'

Gerald shut his paper.

'You'll be doing us all a favour. Go on then, get on with it. What are you waiting for?'

Ivy lunged, more drunk than purposeful, and Gerald blocked the arm holding the knife. Calmly, pleasurably, he drew back his right arm, clenched his hand into a fist and pushed it into Ivy's face. Ivy groaned as she sank to the floor where she stayed, sobbing and whimpering as Gerald walked out of the living-room towards the bedroom.

'Just leave me alone,' he said quietly.

Frances had come back from the bombsite, washed her hair and gone to bed. She knew there was no point in trying to sleep until Gerald got home and the arguing had finished. She lay under the sheet and blankets, muffling the sound of Ivy and Gerald in the warmth of their layers. When there had been a reasonably continuous period of silence she allowed herself to sleep. It must have been very late when Ivy came into her room.

She sensed rather than saw the dark shadow of Ivy standing over her. The sound of the door being opened and then closed had woken her, but something told her not to open her eyes.

Frances separated her eyelids very slightly so that she seemed still to be sleeping and saw Ivy fuzzily through her lashes. Ivy heaved a great sigh or a sob, it was hard to tell which, and dropped her head forward as if it were too heavy for her tired neck. She sat down on the edge of the bed.

'My baby,' she moaned softly, and stroked Frances's cheek with her fingers. 'My baby loves me.'

Frances could smell the alcohol as Ivy breathed the words at her. She knew she couldn't go on pretending to sleep for long, but she was frightened, suddenly, of being alone in the dark with her mother.

Ivy felt swathed in the darkness of the room, as if the night were comforting her with a shawl of shadow dropped gently around her shoulders. The darkness pitied her for her life. Her eyes remained fixed and unblinking on Frances's face in an effort to stop the other grey shapes in the room – pictures, bookshelf, desk, wardrobe – from swirling at the edge of her vision and tipping her off the bed. The upper half of her body rocked in tiny circles around a central point of balance that she couldn't quite find.

'Look at you,' she mumbled. 'Fast asleep. Everybody's asleep. No one'll wake up and talk to me.'

Frances opened her eyes and tried to look half-asleep. She was fully awake now, alert like a dog that senses danger but can't locate it. Ivy's face was smeared with lines of tear-soaked mascara, one eye was swollen out of shape from the blow from Gerald's fist. Her lips dragged, the muscles loosened by alcohol. Frances attempted a sleepy, inconsequential voice.

'Mummy? Tired. Got school tomorrow.'

Ivy inhaled a sob, drawing her tears back into her painful, congested face.

'What have I got tomorrow? Who cares what I want? He lies there sleeping, when he's here. You lie there sleeping. And what about me? What about me? I'm your mother. Look what he's done to me.'

She sniffed back more tears, her mouth set in a half-moon of despair. Frances lay in bed, looking at Ivy, wondering what she was supposed to do. Ivy released the tears she had been saving and allowed them to flow, rocking her sore eye and cheek in her hand as she moaned.

'Nobody cares about me. Nobody loves me. I know, I'm old and ugly. Who would want me? But once . . . once . . .'

She snatched at the bedclothes that covered her daughter. Frances tried to pull them back over her, but Ivy tore them out of her hand and flung them angrily down to the bottom of the bed. Her voice changed to a contemptuous sneer.

'You'll get old too one day. You think you're going to be young for ever, but I'm telling you . . . you listen to what your mother tells you . . . you'll get old and no one will want anything to do with you. You don't want to leave it too late. They don't want you for long, my girl. After a bit they look at you and laugh, or yawn and turn over in the bed.' Ivy let out a broken laugh. 'Let's have a look at you. Let me see what all the fuss is about.'

Frances tried to push away her mother's hand as it began to undo the buttons of her pyjama top.

'What are you doing? Don't. Stop it. Please.'

'It's all right,' she soothed, 'you're my little girl. I can look at my little girl if I want to. All young and lovely.'

Ivy pushed aside Frances's pyjama top and began to run her hand over her daughter's exposed chest.

'Nice little breasts. They won't be as big as mine, but they're coming on. Nice little rosebuds, you've got.'

Frances tried to push the hand away. She wanted to call for help, but there was only her father sleeping, and she was more terrified that he'd come into the room than at what her mother was doing to her. This wasn't a game, like the one she played with Stuart. This was desperate and dangerous, but something for which she had no explanation. She felt it would never be daylight again.

Ivy caressed the budding, barely developed breast, kneading it with the tips of her fingers, rubbing the palm of her hand against the nipple that began to grow under the stimulation.

'Please stop,' Frances begged, frightened by her mother, and scared of the twinge she began to feel in her stomach. 'Don't, Mummy, don't do that.'

'Silky and soft,' Ivy whispered to herself. 'Just like I was. My lovely baby.'

Frances bit hard on her upper lip and began to cry. She felt sick and frightened, dizzy with confusion.

'Don't do that. Please don't.'

Ivy pinched her nipple angrily.

'Don't tell me what to do. I'm your mother.' She smiled a lopsided smile of reassurance and tipped back into tearfulness. 'I wouldn't do anything wrong, I just want to see how my little girl is growing.' Ivy's voice switched again to the miserable whine of a hurt child. 'I just want someone to cuddle.'

She sobbed pitifully for a moment, and then the other voice was back.

'You will too, one day, when nobody wants you any more. I'll show you what happens. Look. Look. That's what becomes of all the loveliness.'

Ivy pulled the belt of her dressing-gown and threw it off. Frances turned her head away and closed her eyes, still sobbing quietly.

'Look. I said, look!' Ivy demanded, and jerked her daughter's face round with her fingers. 'This is what happens when you grow old and no one loves you.'

Ivy grasped the hand that Frances was trying to push her away with and pulled it towards her sagging breast. Frances was enveloped in the sour smell of her mother's alcohol-tinged sweat. She felt the texture of Ivy's fallen breast, cold and clammy against her own sweating palm, the soft, toneless feel of the loose skin on her fingers, like the flesh of cold, dead poultry. Ivy's breasts, usually cupped and firmed inside a brassière, hung heavily down to her waist, dropped like a dead weight against her sagging torso. Ivy held Frances's hand against her with her own, and made it, puppet-like, scoop up the breast beneath it, like an empty bag, into her palm. She kept Frances's hand in place, covered by her own, and made it rotate against her gathered flesh, feeling an old excitement building in her. For a moment she held the hand in place, moaning slightly, willing it to move on her body of its own volition. But, all the time, the hand struggled against her, fighting to get away.

'No, no, don't stop,' she murmured, pressing it harder to her but Frances's hand stayed stiff and resistant, pulling away.

She pushed Frances's hand from her breast and let her own hand take its place, stroking and caressing herself while Frances grabbed the blankets and pulled them tight around her, watching curled up with terror as her mother slipped her other hand between her thighs. Ivy rocked back and forth making a low, sobbing sound, and whispering, 'You think I don't want things? You think I don't have feelings? You love me, don't you? It doesn't matter about him, we've got each other, haven't we? You'll be nice to me, won't you?'

'You're late,' Stuart called as Frances climbed over the rubble to their meeting place inside the wall the next afternoon.

Frances shrugged. Stuart looked agitated. He had been worried that she wouldn't come. He had something to tell her.

'They're going to start building here. I heard my mum talking about it.'

Frances sat on her seat of four bricks and looked up as Stuart spoke.

'What are they going to build?'

'I dunno. I mean we won't be able to come here.'

'We can go to the park.'

'It's not the same. We wouldn't be alone like we are here. This is our place, isn't it?' He was disappointed at her lack of concern. 'Don't you mind?'

Frances shrugged again and began picking at the elastic in one leg of her knickers. Stuart was standing close to her, scraping at a tuft of grass with the toe of his lace-up.

'Well, I mind,' he said, keeping his eyes fixed on the tuft of grass. He kicked the tuft out of the ground and sniffed. 'I love you,' he mumbled. He still hadn't raised his eyes.

Frances looked up sharply and narrowed her eyes.

'Don't be silly. You're being silly.'

'Well, I do.'

'Stupid.'

'It's not.'

'It is.'

'It's not.'

'Well, then I'm glad they're going to build here.'

Frances got up and went to the wall. She picked up a brick from the top row, and threw it into the rubble beyond the empty patch of ground.

'Don't . . .' Stuart jumped over the wall to retrieve the brick, but she picked up another and threw it in a different direction.

'Don't,' Stuart wailed, running for the other brick.

'It's my wall, I'll do what I like.' She kicked a whole section out.

'It's ours. It's our place. Don't. Please don't.'

'It isn't anything. It's just an old bombed-out site. It's just a place.'

Stuart tried to rebuild the wall, putting bricks back on top of each other, while Frances walked purposefully around the inside perimeter and demolished sections of it with her feet.

'Stop it!' Stuart yelled. 'Stop it!'

Frances turned towards him. She was quite calm and even had a small smile on her face. She spoke with careful and complete sincerity.

'I . . . don't . . . care . . . a . . . fuck.'

For a second Stuart simply stared, his hand poised over the wall to replace the brick he'd picked up. The quiet conviction in her voice left no room for persuasion. She looked back at him unblinking.

'Well, neither do I,' he yelled suddenly and flung the brick as far as he could into a pile of rubble. 'I don't give a fuck for this shitty, filthy, cunt, bastard place. Fuck it. I don't care,' he shouted, kicking and heaving at the toppling bricks. 'Girls are rubbish. Girls are stupid. Girls stink!'

Frances shrugged lightly and made her way to the neat pile of clothes by the edge of the site. She didn't look back at Stuart, though she could hear the clunking sound of brick falling and breaking against brick, and his curses carrying harmlessly in the air.

The Peppers had moved into the restricted channel of inevitability. The course of Ivy and Gerald's life had been predictable from the moment they met, but the path had so narrowed that there was no space any longer even for fantasies. They marched on to where they had to go because there was no alternative, no chance now of turning round. But, in truth, there never had been. It's easy to see in retrospect that their hopes and misapprehensions had never been anything more than phantoms on the road. Just as easy to have seen it all along, if you weren't them. Nothing would have helped, not success, not money, not rescue; at best those things would have changed the landscape but not the destination. They were unfinished people given charge of something they could not deal with – their own lives. There was nothing unusual about them, it was the way of much of the world. The odd thing was that, while the world regarded physical disability as a tragedy, it failed, it seemed, to notice the destructive power of less material incapacity.

More often than not, now, Ivy needed tables and the tops of chairs to cross the living-room. Gerald, when he was there, sat slumped in his chair taking grim satisfaction in her decay. He had given up all hope now of finding a way out; he saw in the mirror that he was an ageing, unappetising man, grown fat with discontent. His only pleasure was in watching the more rapid decline of his wife.

'Look at her, the fat, drunken bitch,' he would say, to Frances if she happened to be in the room, to Ivy as she flung slurred abuse at him, to no one in particular if there was no one there. 'I could have been something. I'd have done something, if I hadn't had her on my back.'

It was his only comfort for the fact that he was going to die sooner rather than later without being able to think of a single reason why he had been alive.

Ivy and Gerald blamed each other for something they never

would have had anyway. It was, by now, what kept them together. They had, you might say, a relationship.

And Frances? Frances took what she had learned from her parents: from Ivy, the protection afforded by attention to externals, politeness, correctness, an impregnable surface; from Gerald, disconnection, uninvolvement, the capacity not to be there whether you were there or not.

Ivy remained just effective enough to keep Frances looking respectable on the street. It still mattered to her how the outside world regarded Frances who was her representative in the world. The qualities of a lady were still necessary, the ballet classes went on. Frances was the last tiny chink of hope in Ivy's dark life. There was still the possibility of a good marriage and the mother-in-law's reward for having produced so suitable a daughter. She imagined a large house in the suburbs and the rich, successful man who owned it – something in the city, a merchant banker – insisting she come and live with them; they needed her. She thought about the colour scheme for her room and the weight of the velvet curtain that would hang from the dining-room window during the dinner parties presided over by . . . well, by her daughter, naturally, but everyone would know that behind the elegant wife and the well-run house was the mother.

Gerald had run out of fantasies altogether. The few deals he had managed to arrange since the war were getting fewer and more desperate. He had always operated in a legal no man's land, but now he functioned as a middle-man in arrangements that took him too far from the border to step back over it when the law glanced his way. Investigations began, at first, at some distance from him, but they came closer. An official from the Inland Revenue made polite enquiries. Someone connected with someone he had dealt with was arrested. The someone he had dealt with was interviewed by the police. Gerald wasn't important enough to be protected. He hadn't even done very well out of the deal. He hadn't, he felt, done very well out of anything.

Frances answered the door late one afternoon to a uniformed policeman, his helmet clutched to his chest. He paused for a moment before he spoke, as if he hadn't planned to see a child.

'Is your mother in?'

'She's lying down. She's got a headache.'

'I have to see her. Can you fetch her for me?'

Frances went into the bedroom to wake Ivy.

Ivy stumbled out of bed and tried to brush her hair into something fit for visitors.

'Mrs Ivy Pepper?'

She nodded, numb with fright that the neighbours may have seen the policeman at her door.

'Yes. Come in. Come inside.' She took him by the sleeve and pulled him through the entrance, turning to Frances as she guided him into the living-room. 'Frances, how could you leave him standing at the door like that? Don't you know how to behave? Haven't I always told you?'

Ivy turned back to the policeman, beginning to apologize for her daughter.

'Mrs Pepper, I'm afraid . . . Do you think the little girl could go and make a cup of tea or something . . . I think I ought to speak to you alone.'

Frances left the room reluctantly and put the kettle on, straining to hear the conversation in the next room over the sound of running water.

The policeman spoke too low, his words an awkward official murmur. Frances could catch nothing of what he said. But she heard the sudden cry from Ivy, a wail of shock, then, after some more diffident male mumbling, Ivy's sudden grating squawk of laughter.

'That bastard,' Frances heard. 'The bastard did it on purpose to get at me. The cowardly bastard, I'll get him. I'll get him . . .' The words disappeared into shrieking sobs and the door opened. The policeman looked panic-stricken.

'I think your mum needs a hot cup of tea,' he said. 'What's the name of your family doctor, love? Where's your telephone book?'

Frances pointed to the telephone by the door, almost more alarmed by the look of inadequacy on the policeman's face, than the cries from the next room.

'What's happened?' She stood holding a tea-towel in her hand, staring at the uniformed man who stared back, helplessly at her. They looked at each other in silence for a moment.

'What's happened, please? Why do you need the doctor?'

He took a deep breath. Even to Frances he looked absurdly young. His uniform was intended to impress from a distance, to convey authority to those inclined to challenge it, but it lacked the power to convince close to. The young man beneath the clothes was pitifully ill-equipped for this sort of thing. 'They should have sent a WPC,' he muttered angrily to himself under his breath.

Frances waited.

'It's your dad. He's had an accident.'

Ivy appeared in the doorway, her mouth working, the lips contorting with hate.

'He didn't have any accident. He's tried to do himself in. Gassed himself in the car, but he made sure it wouldn't work. He did it right outside these very flats, so someone would see him. If the bastard wanted to kill himself why didn't he do it properly and hang himself in some dark hole, like the rat he is, where no one could see? I'll tell you why, because he didn't want to die, he doesn't have the guts, he just wanted to make my life more of a misery.'

She jabbed her finger at Frances and spat the words at her as if each phrase were the abracadabra of a spell. Even the thought of the neighbours hearing didn't make her lower her voice.

'I wish he'd really done it. I wish he was dead, and I'd be rid of the bastard.' She turned to the constable. 'Tell him to try again, and this time do it properly.'

The constable stepped between Frances and Ivy.

'Mrs Pepper, please, you're upset. Come and sit down. That's it. Now you stay there quietly and I'll call the doctor. Have you got a drop of whisky in the house?'

Ivy sat in the armchair and sobbed while Frances showed him where the drink was kept.

'Don't worry, love. She's just upset. The doctor'll give her something to calm her down.'

But he was visibly shaken and looked as though he could do with a drink himself. He knew people reacted in all sorts of ways to shock, but Ivy's way was new to him. It wasn't right . . . and with the child there, as well. He'd joined the force to chase criminals up dark alleyways, not for this.

Frances hadn't joined anything, not willingly. No one had sought her consent. She couldn't understand why everyone found it so difficult to leave. Ivy and Gerald threatened to die or kill each other daily as an escape from their intolerable existence, but neither ever succeeded. She was persuaded by their arguments, but still things went on, dangerous and threatening, but never finally coming to an end. Frances couldn't figure out what they were waiting for. She lived in a state of terror: that her life would be blown apart, and that it wouldn't. She began to develop a deep and terrible panic that nothing would ever come to an end.

If she had had a brother or sister, or even a dog, she might have looked for comfort. She might have found solace in the sharing of trouble. Might, even, have identified the pain she felt as pain. But it is the lot of an only child to make interior journeys and find inner landscapes that must be peopled with shadows, rather than make direct connections with the world of flesh and blood. This isn't necessarily a loss, but it is a difference.

Only in her dark, candle-lit sanctuary, where she spent more and more of her time, was there relief from her terror that everything would go on for ever. Down there, she found that other child untouched by the external world, and together they built a model for survival. It centred around the notion she had already developed of wickedness. Frances gradually uncovered its essential quality, the distinguishing flavour that permeated her after her encounters with Stuart, and made her weak with the recognition of her own strength. The acts themselves were of no significance, she began to understand. They were no more than catalysts. Being bad wasn't about doing wrong – not as such. It wasn't about active behaviour at all, except that it often served as a necessary preliminary, because it enabled her to refuse.

Refusal was the real point. Refusal to tell, refusal to allow anyone to know what she knew. Badness, at its vital core, was an act of passivity.

She had learned from watching others that actual misbehaviour was more often used for quite different purposes: for the pleasures of confession and the relief of absolution, which could only be achieved, after all, by an act of wrongdoing. Who could feel themselves an integrated and valued member of society unless there was some way of falling short of the requirements? There was no possibility of the satisfaction of returning to the warmth of the fold unless the requirements for being in it specified what you had to do to be rejected.

It struck Frances with the sudden clarity of enlightenment that this was the point of Goodness. It wasn't a thing in itself, but a way of inventing the Badness that gives Goodness its value. Goodness built the fences, but Badness kept them in good condition.

Wasn't Ivy always showing her that? White gloves were necessary *because* they were impossible to keep clean. It was white gloves dirtied that Ivy looked for because they sat at the centre of the emotional web that tied life together. When the gloves were soiled, there was anger: the pleasing mixture of rage and a sense of virtue as Ivy scrubbed them clean, yet again, knowing they would be marked once more, perhaps irreparably, with oil or blood. For Frances there was the despair of knowing the impossibility of keeping white gloves clean, but that certainty contained the security of knowing that the web would be kept intact. And for both there was the pleasure of punishment and forgiveness when, after the shouting and the withdrawn silence, a tentatively friendly smile was met with something not unfriendly in return. But still, even then, and always, there was the final pleasure of the immediate terror of the next incident of soiled gloves. If not today, then tomorrow; at the very latest, the day after. It would all, inevitably, go on.

Clean, white gloves weren't the point in all this. It was dirty gloves that mattered.

What Frances was after was not to be found in getting the gloves dirty, though that was necessary (and unavoidable) to achieve the end. Her only access to power, the real wickedness, was in not participating in the process of dirty gloves. The gloves had to be soiled, the pantomime of ensuing danger, punishment and forgiveness had to be played out, in order for her, deep in her candle-lit self, *not to care about any of it*.

But she realised slowly that this didn't go far enough. Refusal could be taken a step further.

The model she built with the bad girl was made, like all good models, with what was to hand. She imagined two pairs of gloves: an official pair of white gloves, a public, apparent pair, but also another pair, filthy, never washed, torn. These were the ones she wore when Ivy wasn't looking; a pair of gloves so disreputable that wearing them was an absurdity. Bare hands, clean beneath the foul and tattered cotton, would have been preferable, but were not to be preferred. These secret gloves that Ivy would never know about completely negated the pristine pair Frances seemed to be wearing. Because the official gloves were hardly ever worn they remained white, their appearance was maintained and all the knots of relationship that had been tied by the anger and pleasure, the confession and forgiveness, were undone without anyone, except Frances, ever knowing it had happened.

Frances, you see, was a genuine subversive. She possessed an instinctive understanding of the real nature of power. Not that, then or later, she consciously used or thought in terms of subversion or power. Her private view of herself remained, defined as wickedness. But she knew that her secret self could never be fulfilled by *acts*. Not acts of rebellion, or revolution, or terrorism – in the smallest or largest of their senses. Refusal was the essence, but even that couldn't be just an act of refusal, no mere rejection would do. What she knew, without ever having to put it to herself in so many words (and even here she remained subversive, for a thesis on the subject of subversion would have been a 'doing'), was that any act, positive or negative, was participation. Rules broken remained rules. The chaos of terrorism merely disrupts an order that the terrorist acknowledges by the act of destruction. And something destroyed is something that can be rebuilt. Putting your foot down implies a solid base to put your foot on.

All acts have consequences, and consequences have an effect. Frances's great talent was to be profoundly indifferent to the effect. She couldn't avoid the acts, nor therefore the consequences, but she could refuse the effects that were always the real point, and what kept the story rolling on, connecting and interconnecting.

The candle-lit space inside her was the place where she didn't care, and where she sought refuge from the effects of the doings of herself and others. It was the place where, having said 'no', she could retreat from the results, which inevitably occurred, but mattered not at all down there. But, more crucial, it was the place where, having said 'yes', she could go and, privately, utterly refuse, utterly negate whatever was happening, without anyone knowing. Down there 'yes' and 'no' were rendered impotent, meaningless by the power of her secret refusal. The world thought itself unchanged, but Frances knew better. Frances blew the world away by never letting it know that it had gone.

– I see now why it was that your mother understood and appreciated you as no one else could. You were her finest refusal.

– You *have* been listening. I'm almost proud to have invented you.

– You evidently have a talent for inventing characters to fulfil your needs. What about you, do you take after your mother? Are you a refuser, too?

– Me. What can I refuse? No brain, no choice. You know how it is with me.

– Or are you the ultimate refuser? I don't want to detract from your mother's achievements, but the fact that she had to *choose* refusal taints the non-participation. At least it does if you're going to be perfectionist about it, and you are something of a perfectionist, in your way.

– The ultimate refuser?

– You, unlike Frances, cannot choose to refuse. You *are* refusal. You *are* non-participation. You *are* passivity. Perhaps that's what upsets people about you, the ones who thought you never should have been born. There is nothing they can do about you. There isn't even the possibility of reasoning, bribing, cajoling, threatening you into participation, is there? You're like any arbitrary accident, you make no sense. Frances, in her fashion, made some sense. She had, if only at a half-conscious level, a philosophy, and you can only have *a* philosophy if there are others that you reject. See what I mean – participation?

– I was just telling you a story, just passing . . .

– Don't get me wrong, I'm not setting you up in competition with your mother; she did the best she could, given her handicap. For a fully-brained member of the human race, she did well. But if it's genuine non-participation you're after, you're the one.

– I invented you and a language that can't possibly exist so that I could tell you a story. What could be more participatory than that?

– Well, it's not my place to argue, I know. I'll concede that inventing a language and a listener suggests a *will* to participate. It's a touch active. But that only goes to prove my point – what's the use of a will without a way? What could be more pointless, more negative, than a story that doesn't exist, told in a language that doesn't exist to an auditor that doesn't exist?

– I'm getting tired of your interruptions. I don't even like telling stories, it was just a way of passing the time. I'll stop now.

– Look, take no notice of me. What do I know? I'm nothing but a pair of ears. It would be a shame to stop now. I'll keep my comments to myself.

– You have no right to have any comments. You weren't designed to think, only to listen.

– Trouble is, things seem to take on a life of their own once they're invented. Tell me the story.

– No. I could abolish you if I wanted to.

– I know. Tell me the story.

– Only if you stop interrupting and making comments.

– I'll try, but it won't be easy. I've grown to like conversing with you.

– Well, don't. Anyway, you should treat me with respect. I'm a tragedy. People don't converse with tragedies, they avert their gaze.

– But I'm not people, am I? And you're not a tragedy. You can't feel or experience, you don't have any problems. At best, you're your mother's tragedy, but I've got reservations even about that.

– Oh?

– Look at it from your mother's point of view. There are considerable advantages to a baby like you, you know. You won't, for example, grow out of more than two or three sets of clothes. She'd never have to worry about the correct development of your feet. Do your shoes fit properly, is there enough width, are the arches correctly supported? You know, the kind of thing that causes parents to travel considerable distances to find a shoe shop with a decent fitting service. You don't wear shoes, you never will. No mother would ever have to fret about your schooling, or argue with you about staying out late, or worry about how far you've gone and whether she ought to have the whole business of contraception out with you. She wouldn't even have to be granny to your kids. You're a short-term proposition, not a long-term burden. There's a lot to be said for you, when you come to think of it.

– If I'm not a tragedy, what am I?

– What does it matter? What do you care? You're just passing the time.

– You took the words right out of my mouth.

– Imaginary mouth.

– Quite. Shall I continue or would you rather spend the rest of my life in contemplative silence?

– No, I'm a dedicated listener.

– Well, you could have fooled me. You do a lot of interrupting, considering.

– Intervals are important. Us listeners need the occasional break. What a lonely child she was, your mother.

– She had her phantom friend in her inner landscape, her internal mirror.

– But it was a mirror in which she could only see her own reflection.

– What else is there to see in mirrors? As a child and as an adult Mother looked at herself all the time, one way or another. In mirrors, in passing windows of shops, cars and houses. And people's eyes. It gave people the impression that when she looked at them she was really looking. Which goes some way to account for the disappointment, even betrayal, that some people experienced with her. It seemed to them that she implied or promised a connection that never materialised. In fact all she was doing was to examine herself in their eyes. Mother was ever the subject of misunderstanding.

– What was she looking for?

90

– What she saw. The curved image of herself that other eyes received and brains interpreted. A picture of herself that assured her she was there to be seen.

– What did she see when she looked into your eyes?

– I was different. My eyes, after all, are baby-blue. They reflect poorly in the normal way. But if other people reflected what they thought she was, I bounced back at her what she knew about herself. The image of her emptiness. I provided the most convincing version of herself. Empty physicality, her greatest secret. I showed her she was substance without substance. The others showed her that she hadn't been found out but, with me, she could be herself.

– You provided a real service.

– She appreciated me, there's no doubt of that. She told me one evening after my bath. She lifted a curl of my hair with her hand and ran the soft brush along it until it fell back into place. She loved my hair. 'What you are is all there is to fight for, Nony,' she said, 'just life, pure physical existence. That's all there was at first, you know. After the Big Bang, and the eons it took to create the space between the stars, came molecules of life that did nothing but live. Just like you. Nothing that thought or cared or planned its future. You are what it has always been about. A nothing that lives. Mindless, functionless, just being, not doing or thinking. I wouldn't have you any other way. You are my very own remarkable child.'

– That must have made you feel good.

– Funnily enough, it was as near as I've ever got to experiencing guilt. It's not something I'm naturally prey to. Guilt's a condition that belongs to the developed brain. You can hardly feel guilty if nothing is your fault.

– Oh, these days guilt is of the free-floating variety. You don't have to *do* anything to be saturated with it.

– Still, you need the possibility, at least, of doing something wrong for guilt to have any meaning. And what can I do wrong? Even so, at that moment, as my mother praised me for my existential purity, I felt, well, *something*. As if my ability to take her in, to see and hear her in my peculiar way were a secret that I was withholding. No, not that, because

I wasn't in a position to reveal the truth. But I knew that if I could have spoken, if I could have told my mother how it was with me, I would have kept silent. I wouldn't have had the courage to disappoint her – to become ordinary in her eyes. I wanted to be my remarkable mother's remarkable child.

– An extraordinarily human piece of logic, if I may say so.

– Not me, not human.

– What could be more human than feeling bad about something you might not do, knowing you couldn't do it anyway? It's so wonderfully theoretical, it can only be described as human.

– Must be in the blood. Do you like the sound of my mother, so far?

– Not much. You make her sound interesting, but not very likeable.

– I don't *make* her anything. She is what she is. Count yourself lucky that she's interesting or you'd have had a very boring time of it. Very few people appreciated her the way I do.

– Stuart seems to have appreciated her.

– Alas, poor Stuart.

– You knew him well?

– Depends what you mean by 'know'. Naturally I didn't know him. I don't know anyone. You seem to forget my condition.

– It does occasionally slip my mind. But I can rely on you to remind me.

– Perhaps if you concentrated instead of asking questions . . . I don't have all the time in the world, you know.

– You have all the time in your world. What more do you need?

– Your silence.

– I'm entirely at your service. Please continue with your story.

– It's my mother's story. But she doesn't need it any more. I'm just borrowing it to pass the time. I don't think I like you.

– It doesn't matter. I'm all you've got in the way of an audience. You invented your imagined language to tell the story; what do you care who listens?

– You're right. I'll go on, but you keep quiet, or I'll settle for oblivion.

– Atta girl.

FRANCES WAS WELL on her way to becoming her own particular and remarkable self.

She kept her refusals to herself for the next few years; she said 'yes' quietly and peaceably to the world although every nod was noted and tagged with an angry candle in the place where 'no' sat in exile, waiting.

She passed her eleven plus, or rather failed to fail it, and started at the local grammar school. Navy-blue gymslip, white shirt with the top button done up, a navy and maroon striped tie. And, for outdoors, a navy beret and blue-belted mackintosh. Her gloves became woollen and navy for everyday wear, but the socks stayed white and neatly turned down at the top. White socks, in an average school day, were just as hard to keep clean as white gloves, so nothing was really lost. The first few days bewildered Frances as they did everyone else – she was at the bottom of the school now, and still very hesitant – but before long she discovered that there was a boiler-house here too, although in this particular case it was the bicycle sheds and sometimes the lavatories. She noted them and the style and demeanour of those older pupils who drifted in that direction during break-time.

In the meantime, she taught herself to smoke on her journeys to and from school, since by then sex, cigarettes and sin were inextricably linked and you either did it – smoke, and therefore everything else – like Marlene Dietrich, or you didn't and ended up marrying Rock Hudson. Even if Frances hadn't wanted to be bad, the times were such that it would have taken a very strong stomach to be good.

Apart from that her behaviour caused no concern. She sat quietly at the back of the class and produced satisfactory work when required. There was nothing that anyone could complain about. Like the clean gloves she kept for Ivy, her

94

outward behaviour allayed suspicion and allowed her the deep inner satisfaction of knowing how little they knew. And if the dirty gloves were kept, at this time, mostly in her pocket, she knew they were there when she wanted them.

Frances's refusal to care was like an unused muscle that needed to be developed with deliberate and careful exercise. To the world looking on, the exercise is evident and looks like an activity in itself, but the underlying reality – the strengthening muscle – is the real point and, at first, invisible to the observing eye. For a while, though, even the exercise was hard to observe. Her progress on the road signposted 'Disaster' was slow at first, but she had, at least, identified her route. Once she was sure it would take her where she intended to go, there was no great hurry; she had only to put one foot in front of the other, and follow the signs the dying decade thoughtfully placed for uncertain travellers.

The old bombsite had been screened with hoardings and cleared, and a new concrete and glass edifice had emerged from the rubble. Everyone – well, almost everyone – said how smart and modern it looked. The times were beginning to change, little by little.

Stuart was in his fourth year at the grammar school, but Frances didn't recognize him. Two years in a young life is so long that the memory is as hazy as senility. In any case, he was hardly the same boy she had known only a couple of years before on the bombsite. His hormones had wrenched the boyishness away and thrown up instead a youth, high-rise and modern, like the building that now replaced the bombsite. His school blazer and satchel were as pathetically ineffectual a disguise as a plainclothes policeman still wearing his regulation boots. Growth spurted from every pore, leaving his clothes looking exhausted with the attempt to catch up. But the sudden rush of hormones had done nothing to alter his eyes which, when he recognised her during assembly, glowered at the back of Frances's head with the same sullen, resentful longing they had expressed the first time and the last time they met. Frances had grown too, of course, but not in so transforming a way.

Stuart watched her surreptitiously and morosely from a

distance when he saw her coming and going about the school, but he never spoke to her. They were placed in the social and spatial geography of the world now. When they had known each other before it was in the private, sealed world of the bombsite, knickers and trousers down, engaged in a mutual exploration. Now the public world and its requirements kept them separate. Fourteen-year-old boys don't want to be seen talking to twelve-year-old girls. Frances wasn't even especially pretty. She was curiously striking, a kind of long-necked bird, swan-featured, camouflaged by blue serge, but she didn't have the sort of looks that made Stuart and his friends pass noisy, aggressive remarks in the street.

It was to be almost two years before he spoke to her. Frances knew him by sight, but still didn't connect him with the boy she had known. He wore glasses now, and although he had a group of friends in the lower-sixth he was quieter than most of them, a little solitary even when they were all together strutting their top-of-the-heap status as near-adults. He was considered bright by his teachers, and doing several science A levels that would, it was agreed, assure him of a good career in electronics or engineering. To Frances, in the third year, the lower-sixth were known from a distance, and Stuart, sitting studying in the library, or popping in to discuss something with the teacher during a physics lesson, made a less dramatic impression than most. He wasn't handsome, but he had a rather grown-up look, partly as a result of his glasses, that made him seem in turn unusually thoughtful or severe.

Frances wasn't part of a group. She had made friends with a girl in her class who had also remained outside the parties that had been formed in the first few terms at the school. Sandra and Frances went around together at first, by default, because they were both loose elements in the grouping of the form, but the pairing held together, though they weren't obviously suited.

While Frances worked just hard enough to keep things ticking over and acceptable, Sandra slaved to produce love and admiration. She wanted more than anything in the world to gain her teachers' approval and her parents' pride, but always failed, somehow, to reach the degree of excellence that would have marked her out as exceptional. She admired Frances's open contempt for the way she tried, spending hours over an essay, dizzy with fear and expectation as the teacher handed the exercise books back around the class, only to find another B minus at the bottom, and the usual comment, 'A good effort.' They didn't even write, 'You could do better.' Sandra's efforts were extreme, but she only ever managed to do as well as expected.

'Why do you care so much?' Frances would ask, as Sandra wept over a returned piece of homework in the cloakroom. 'B minus is OK.'

'I want an A,' Sandra hiccuped. 'I want to go home with an A. I want them to be proud of me.'

Sandra's real, God-given talent was her looks. Getting a B minus took everything she had, but even the deliberate drabness of her school uniform could do nothing to hide her lush beauty. Frances, still the scrawny, adolescent duckling, thought it amazing that someone should have been given every desirable physical attribute. Some people were pretty, but fat; others with perfect legs had hair that nothing could be done about; the prettiest *retroussé* nose could be spoiled just a little by crooked teeth. The most attractive people seemed to have some compensating flaw that made others feel better about them. But there was nothing about Sandra that wasn't exactly as anyone would wish for themselves. She was an exemplar of the way females were supposed to look as 1959 became the Sixties.

As Sandra dropped her head to blow her nose, her sand-gold hair tumbled forward, the curls magically awry, as if each had been carefully arranged to fall just so by an artist who understood the appeal of the perfectly haphazard. The already limpid eyes swam, and glistened hugely with unshed tears, held in check by the halo of long lashes. Her nose wasn't even red, just pretty. Her breasts were already formed, her fingers fine and delicate, her legs . . . There was nothing that wasn't just right about her. Frances marvelled at Nature's bull's-eye as they sat on the narrow wooden bench in the forest of limp navy-blue macs that hung all round them. There wasn't a boy in the school whose eyes didn't hunger as Sandra came into view and passed them without a glance, too used to the look, and too preoccupied with getting an A, to notice or care.

'Why do you mind so much? B minus is fine.'

'My brother got A plus for everything. He's going to come down from Balliol with a double first.'

'What's a double first?'

'I don't know. It's like A plus, but better. My mother says I'm letting the family down. They were going on at me the other night over dinner. Mummy said it was a pity I wasn't plainer because then I might be cleverer. And my father said that if I were plainer I'd probably only be getting C's. Then they laughed and shook their heads and Mummy said that maybe, the way things were, at least I might manage to marry someone clever.'

'What did you say?'

'Nothing. I left the table and went and cried in my room. But I don't think they noticed I'd gone.'

'Well, don't mind.'

'You don't mind, but I'm not like you. I envy you. You really don't care. You're so brave, I wish I were like you.'

Frances wondered why she wanted to cry suddenly.

'Take no notice of them. Shall I help you with your essays?'

Sandra looked up.

'But you only get B's for yours.'

'Yes, but I don't try very hard. I could get A's if I wanted to.'

'But, if you can, why don't you get them for yourself?'

Frances pulled one side of her mouth into a dismissive smile.

'I don't want to, but I don't mind getting them for you, if it'll help.'

Frances felt confused when she listened to Sandra talk about her family. She could see it from Sandra's point of view, how horrible she must feel, how miserable she obviously was, but, still, she liked to hear about her mother and father, the conversations over dinner, the family visits to Oxford to see Sandra's brother, the family-ness, the normality of it all. She liked the idea of her high marks gaining their praise, even if they were on Sandra's essays. And she did want to cheer Sandra up too.

'Would you?' Sandra looked excitedly at Frances, who shrugged.

'Yeah, why not?'

They took it gradually, working up to the A's, through the alphabet and its gradations.

'You don't want to get good too suddenly, or they'll be suspicious,' Frances explained. Sandra nodded gratefully. By the time she was getting A regularly (with the occasional A minus for authenticity), Frances's marks had dropped to an average C. She didn't mind, and nobody noticed the coincidence. Sandra came to school increasingly bright-eyed. As if, thought Frances, they weren't bright enough already. But she enjoyed hearing about the surprise of Sandra's parents, and their praise over the dinner table.

The distant, misplaced praise pleased Frances much more than A's of her own and pats on her own back would have. She could have done well, if she wanted, but she chose not to. No one would ever know.

But Sandra's bright eyes didn't hold their new light for long. The novelty of her marks wore off. In some way, they made things worse than before; now what wasn't good enough about her had no focus. No one actually named her failure; it simply sat in the air between her mother and father, like a looming cloud, darkening the room, a permanent twilight that was worse because it was irremediable. It was *her* they couldn't stand, not something particular she could do anything about. She was a girl; she was little more than a child, with eyes that couldn't help looking as if she had just left her lover's bed; she moved like a country slut, with a wantonness that was made worse by her complete lack of intention. She disturbed and distressed her parents who felt they could do no more than temporarily maintain a holding operation on their changeling offspring. The son was their child, the pride of their genes. His brains, intelligence, quickness were reflections of the quality of the parents, of their own capacities and the environment they provided. The loose sensuality of their daughter was none of their doing and they didn't like it, or her, and never would. If she was only capable of getting a C on her own, without the help of Frances or her looks, it was because they had shown her time and again that that was all she could hope for. In some unspoken way, they all knew the A's did not belong to her because they had deprived her of them years ago.

Outside home, Sandra was, as her parents feared, an unwitting object of lust. She wasn't interested, she wanted something else, but Frances was kept busy as handmaiden to the goddess. She was forever receiving notes asking her to ask Sandra if she would go out with the writer. Boys would stop her in the corridor or get other girls to be friendly with her to get to Sandra. Sandra went out with some of them, allowed them to walk home with her, and sometimes to sneak kisses, or put their hands up her jumper. She was in no sense promiscuous, she went out with one boy at a time. It was just that there was always someone waiting to take his place when he went too far and wanted too much. Sandra became used to being wanted in the way she was; indeed she would have found it strange if there had been a gap which no one was waiting to fill.

Frances was used to it, too, fitting herself between Sandra's boyfriends, listening to her shifting moods about this one or that. So when Stuart approached them one lunch-time as they sat together on a bench in the playground, she wasn't surprised, although she rated his chances lower than most. She had noticed him hanging around in their vicinity for some time. Now he sat down next to Sandra. Frances felt a little sorry for him, Sandra had too much choice to get involved with someone so reserved. He began a conversation in low whispers. Sandra bent her head towards him and answered him quietly. Frances opened the book she had beside her. After a few moments Stuart left.

'He wants me to ask you if you'll go out with him,' Sandra said.

'Don't be silly. It's you he's after.'

'No, honestly. He said would I talk to you. He wants to meet you after school.'

'Why?' Frances was astonished.

'I don't know. He likes you, I suppose,' Sandra quite enjoyed her new role as negotiator.

'Rubbish, he probably wants to talk to me about you.'

'I don't think so, not from the way he talked. Why not meet him and see?'

'I'm not interested in boyfriends. Anyway, I don't believe it, it's some kind of trick. Boys aren't interested in me.'

Sandra shrugged.

'Well, this one is.'

Stuart waited at the gates at the end of the day. Frances approached him briskly and was short with him, in spite of their difference in age. Sixth-formers usually expected and got a degree of deference from the lower school.

'What do you want?'

'Let's walk.'

'I go this way,' she said, pointing and hoping that it was the wrong direction.

'I know.'

They began to walk. They both kept their heads down, eyes towards the pavement. Stuart clutched a small pile of textbooks to his chest. In the silence Frances began to feel Stuart's discomfort. It was more than that; there was a strong sense of pain in his muteness, an awkwardness that approached agony. He had none of the brash confidence of the older boys who came to her to intercede for them with Sandra. Her own confusion about why he should be walking with her, and in such pain, was increased.

'What do you want?'

'I . . . er . . . I want . . . Don't you remember the bombsite?' he blurted out.

Frances stopped and looked at him. Suddenly she recognized him.

'You built the wall with me . . .'

'We used to meet, every day. Remember?'

She began to remember. But it was private, her own memory. She was annoyed to realize that the recollection

101

was not hers alone. The boy on the bombsite hadn't been the point; Stuart then, and especially now, had nothing to do with it. He was an interloper. She felt as if a stranger had read her private diary and knew too much about her. A rage boiled up from that place in her that was hers alone, and exploded.

'Go away. Leave me alone.'

She turned and walked quickly away from him, making a distance between them that rendered them strangers on the same street.

Stuart had no choice but to follow Frances. It wasn't the way it was with his friends, not the way everything he knew about the world suggested it should be, but Stuart *had* fallen in love with Frances on the bombsite. He had cried it out to her when he was twelve, the last time they met, when he should have been too young to mean it. But he had. The words, that some men never speak or mean during their whole lives, were the only ones that fitted what had happened to him. Frances had gouged a wound in him that had never gone away, and that he knew would be with him for as long as he lived. It wasn't the masturbation, it was her. For three years he had lived with her image permanently engraved on his mind. In the background of his thoughts, no matter what they were, Frances's face floated, plain, strange, the dark eyes cool and querying, the hair, plaited, then loose, the rich red of gemstones and fertile soil. The child that had broken into him, a child himself. He knew it should never have happened, but knew it would never go away. He couldn't understand what it was or why it was. He had gone out with a girl or two, and done as much as adolescent boys can do with adolescent girls, but always there was Frances, sitting quietly in his head, pressing on his heart, staring quizzically, not quite laughing at his inability to forget her.

He hadn't ever spoken about it to anyone, of course. How could he? His friends would laugh at his unimaginable problem. They masturbated, singly or in groups, and discussed their degrees of success with willing girls. Their aims in life were to pass their A levels and to penetrate. Love was a word spoken only by girls to frustrate them or by nineteenth-century authors that had to be studied because they were on the syllabus. Love, in the first case, was something to be circumvented and, in the second, to be discussed as a theme with reference to its different manifestations in the characterization of Othello, Desdemona and Iago.

Stuart's father had died long ago, and love, according to his mother, was expressed by the struggle she had had since to keep Stuart fed and clothed. She had worked herself into old age by the time she was forty, forgoing her own pleasures, lost now and unimaginable, to devote herself to her son. Life was hard and grim, and that, if he had asked, would be his mother's definition of love. Girls were distractions; he owed her success, a good career, not heartache for the image of a little girl.

Stuart watched Frances go into the entrance of her block of flats and felt the desperation that belongs to a need not under control. The day would never come when he wouldn't mind seeing Frances walk away from him. He was appalled that such a thing should have happened, but clear that it had and that nothing would save him.

The child that sat in the centre of Frances's inner space had lost patience with waiting. She wanted something to happen, anything, so long as it was strong and final. It was time. There had been enough comfort.

Frances knew that something had gone wrong. The space inside had contracted and she seemed to have forgotten how to enlarge it. The rage, the cutting fury was all there; she knew the dark candles were blazing with their strange light, but she was excluded. It was no longer a sanctuary she could sit and breathe in quietly and feel there was somewhere she was safe. Her inside place had shut her out and left her outside in the dangerously inconsequential world.

She found herself with nowhere else to go but in the same direction as her parents. The panic she had felt, that they would simply go on and on, sitting in the hate-filled flat waiting for the release of death, suddenly included her too. It crossed her mind, now that she was without her refuge, that she was not immune to the never-endingness, and that it was possible that her life too would slip into the miserable routine of despair. A million moments without hope, leading nowhere. The panic boiled inside her. Better to stop the thing now than find herself where her parents were. Gerald, sunk into a chair, refusing to speak to anyone and muttering to himself about lost opportunities and betrayals. Ivy, tottering more with hatred than drink, still asking, but never answering the question of what had happened to her life. Now, at fourteen and with no inside place to go, Frances could see herself becoming like them. She could leap over the next two decades and find herself in a hate-filled space that held no hope except that it would inevitably end.

She rejected the vision. Either she had to find her way back inside herself, back into the sanctuary, or she needed disaster to save herself from what life was capable of doing to her.

In fact, they were not alternatives. It became clear that there was no way back into her refuge without dispensing with the safety net of hope. She had to *know*, through and through, really believe because it was true, that there was no risk in anything, because there was no hope that could be destroyed. She had to get rid of the fear by rejecting hope.

The small, grinning child inside her wouldn't allow her in, but sat, Buddha-like, in the candlelight and demanded she walk a line that had solid ground only on one side of it. The place she was looking for could only be entered by a sliver of a soul, something that had crossed the boundary of goodness and been stripped of substance. To do that, it seemed she needed to risk and lose everything, to cross firmly into the territory that Sandra, wide-eyed with fear, called 'what's-going-to-become-of-my-life'. She needed to get to that great, empty hole that held no further risks. Once there, there would be nowhere else to go.

'Come on, it'd be easy. We wouldn't get caught.'

Sandra shook her head, and backed away from Frances, at the door of the chemistry lab.

'No. I don't want to. We'd get into terrible trouble. I don't want to.'

The chemistry teacher was bent over the bench elaborating a detail of the lesson that had just ended to two boys whom he felt showed particular promise. Behind him the blackboard was covered with formulae and some of the words that had difficult spellings, and behind that the door of the stockroom stood ajar.

'He'll never see us,' Frances insisted, pulling Sandra slightly by the sleeve.

'No. Anyway,' she whispered, 'what do you want it for?'

'He said it would make you unconscious. We could just try it, to see what it's like. Just for fun.'

'What's the fun in being unconscious? It might be dangerous. And if we got caught, we'd be in real trouble.'

'It's interesting. Oh, come on. It'll be all right. He won't even know it's gone. Please.'

Sandra pulled away from Frances.

'No, I'm not going to,' she said as she walked away and Frances stamped after her. 'I don't want to, and I don't want to get into trouble.'

'What can they do to you, even if they caught us? Just for fun, just for the sake of it.'

'They'd tell my parents. I don't want to get in trouble with my parents. And I don't think it would be fun. He said ether was really dangerous.'

Frances stopped and the two girls faced each other. Frances stared angrily at Sandra.

'You're a rotten friend. Why do you have to be good all the time?'

Sandra looked helpless and slightly ashamed.

'I have to. I have to be good. I don't want to get into . . .'

'Trouble!' Frances sneered. 'The good little girl doesn't want to get into trouble. You're so boring. I don't need you, anyway. I can get the stuff on my own. So you go off to the library like a good girl. I'll go and steal the ether without your help.'

'Don't . . .' Sandra said, frightened now that even her association with Frances would get her into trouble. But her friend had vanished back into the door of the chemistry lab. Sandra walked on quickly towards the library.

Frances was pleased that it had happened. She was fed up with Sandra, who wouldn't smoke in the lavatory at break-time, who worried about being late for lessons, who fussed and feared everything and everyone. Frances was tired of pretending to be good, of being held back by Sandra's anxiety. The place inside her was brimfull of angry candles, ablaze with fury at her own virtue.

'Fuck her,' she said, under her breath, the word acting like oxygen on the flames that sprang higher. 'Fuck them all.'

Inside her a small child opened her eyes and smiled happily at the conflagration. She blinked and smiled with the joy of being awake and full of energy. She wanted to walk along the edge of cliffs, looking down at great waves breaking dangerously against the granite. She wanted to swim too far out to sea and feel the fathoms beneath her holding her up, pulling her down. She wanted to stand at the edge of the road watching fast cars fly past, with only the distance of her stride between each one, and lift one foot off the pavement to take a step. She longed, with all the banked-up energy inside her, to risk everything, to live the second between safety and disaster, perfectly balanced on the pin-point of choice.

Frances was too late. Mr Stokes was just coming out of the stockroom, searching his keyring as he pulled the door shut.

'What is it, Frances? Have you left something behind?'

'Yes. No, it's all right, I've just remembered where I left it.'

'Well, you'd better hurry off to your next lesson, or you'll be late.'

Frances was furious that she'd allowed Sandra's fussing to stop her. The bottle of ether became a grail, but several chemistry lessons went by without another chance to get into the stockroom without being seen. Then she remembered Stuart. She knew Mr Stokes let him potter around in there without supervision. She'd seen him setting up experiments on a side bench during their lessons, walking in and out of the room, getting bottles of acid or whatever he needed. She remembered the bombsite, and the look she had seen in his eyes.

'What the hell do you want with ether?'

'I want to try it. Will you get it for me or won't you?'

'Of course I won't. It's very dangerous, you can kill yourself with that stuff. I'm not going to steal it for you.'

'I thought you liked me.'

'Why?' Stuart was perplexed. 'What do you want to try it for?'

'I want to see what it's like. I want to put myself out and see.'

'Don't be stupid. You have to use tiny quantities. If you use it on yourself you'll get dizzy and you won't be able to control how much you use. You could die.'

'I want it. If you're worried about it, you can do it for me. You can put me out with it. Are you scared or what?'

'I don't want to . . .'

'Please! If you don't I'll do it myself and I'm much more likely to get caught. And I'll take it on my own. It'd be much safer if you helped me. Please!'

Stuart shook his head, but it was clear to Frances that he wasn't refusing to do it.

'If I get some, you'll just try it once? And that's all. OK? And you won't do it on your own? You've got to promise.'

'Yes, I promise. Will you do it, then?' Frances smiled gratefully at him. 'Will you?'

'All right. But you've promised. Just once,' Stuart said, troubled by his fear of losing the smile on the face of the girl in front of him.

Her smile became a beam of pleasure and she threw her arms around him in a hug.

'Oh, I knew you would. Thanks, Stuart.'

He watched her go off to her next lesson, a skinny, angular third-former. It was the first time she had called him by his name.

Frances's instinct about ether was right. It was what it did to time that she had been after.

107

'It's as if you live a whole lifetime,' she explained to Stuart when she came round the first time. 'As if there's another world, deeper down, that takes much longer than this one.'

'But you were only out for two or three minutes,' Stuart told her.

'It didn't feel like that, though, to me. It was much more real, more,' she tried to find a word that worked, 'vivid than when I'm awake.'

'Isn't it just like being asleep and dreaming?'

'Not really. A bit, but not really because there wasn't any story. Not even any me, not like there is in dreams. There was just time, masses and masses of time, as if time was the only inhabitant of that world.'

'Doesn't sound much fun.'

'I loved it. I want to go there again. I'd like to live there. Why don't you try?'

'You promised you'd only do it once.' Stuart picked up the dark-brown bottle and put it in his briefcase.

'I know, but I didn't know how much I'd like it. You can kiss me if you want.'

Stuart was angry.

'You're just using me. You know I like you, and you're using me.'

He looked at Frances accusingly. She sat on the floor of the storeroom, her legs curled under her. Her hair was loose and fell forward in front of her shoulders, thick and shiny even in the dim light that entered from the tiny frosted-glass window. Her eyes were still a little unfocused from the effects of the ether. Stuart squatted in front of her and knew his mind had taken a snapshot of her sitting there that he would have to see every day and for ever. She was no beauty, it wasn't that. It was the challenge in her, that shone from her eyes, that created the urgent tone in her voice, that made the muscles in her long neck seem to quiver with tension and will. Her will to will him to do what she wanted made her an essential part of him. She challenged him at the bombsite, she challenged him to steal and drug her, and she offered him sexual excitement as a way of achieving what she wanted. But it wasn't even what she offered that had the power over him, it was the urgency of her own need, nothing really to do with him at all. It was the strength of what she wanted, and the fact that he didn't understand what that was and knew he didn't know, that made him unable to refuse her. He also wanted to kiss her.

'I don't think I like that much,' she said.

'What?' Stuart braced himself for pain.

'You putting your tongue in my mouth. Do you have to?'

Stuart turned away slightly.

'It's how people kiss.'

'Well, I think it's disgusting. But I've seen it in films.'

'The woman does it back to the man.'

Frances made a face.

'Ugh. I'll let you do it to me if you like it so much, but I'm definitely not going to put my tongue in your mouth, and that's that.'

'You're supposed to enjoy it.'

'I can't see what's enjoyable about it. It's just wet and sloppy, and what's the point?'

Stuart shrugged. Frances took his hand.

'Look, it doesn't matter. I don't mind much. And I like you. Really, I do.'

They used up the bottle of ether in a week, with Stuart always protesting but, in the end, giving Frances what she wanted so badly. He stole another bottle and, when that was finished, worrying that Stokes would notice how much ether had been used recently, bought some from the chemist on the way to school. He explained to the elderly man in the white coat that he was a butterfly collector.

'Not many butterflies around this part of town,' the chemist suggested.

'No, I go to the country at weekends to do my collecting.' He described the killing bottle and the pad of ether-soaked cottonwool at the bottom.

'Poor little things.'

'No, they don't feel anything,' Stuart assured him. 'They don't have enough brain to know what's happening to them.'

'Even so, it seems a shame. Still, I suppose it's good for a lad to have a hobby, at least you don't go ripping up cinema seats.'

Stuart allowed his thick glasses to substantiate his virtue and smiled mildness at the chemist, acknowledging his preference for the destruction of butterflies over the destruction of private property. He handed over half a crown.

'Bye for now,' the chemist nodded, adding, as Stuart went through the door, 'and be careful with that stuff. It can be dangerous if you don't treat it with respect.'

Somewhere around the middle of this bottle, Frances began to scream. The empty place where there was nothing but endless time became populated by monsters. The peace and quiet of absolute nothingness were shattered by malevolent beasts whose size complemented the vastness of the ether universe. They smelt her out, knowing she was there by their very existence. They sought their maker, who had thought herself absent, and heaved towards her, all tendrils, claws and vicious tearing fangs, intent on her destruction. In the dark, deep world of the ether, Frances discovered her own presence and the terror that accompanies existence. There was nothing to do against these beasts but scream into the eons of time.

Stuart was terrified that someone would hear and find them in the storeroom. He shook and stroked Frances back into consciousness.

'Ssh, ssh, be quiet. Frances, wake up, come on. We'll get caught.'

Frances quivered with the memory of the terror and sobbed quietly into Stuart's chest. When she recovered she sat up and wiped the tears from her eyes.

'I'm all right. I don't want to do that any more.'

She refused to explain to Stuart what had happened, but she was low with disappointment for days after. She had found, in those first few sessions, so precisely what she wanted: another place, another time, a kind of extended nothingness where she existed and didn't. Not child or adult, or she or he, just a mind that created a vast empty space and let it be. It was shocking that it had become a place of horror so suddenly. How could there be horror where there was nothing? It was completely unexpected, and now that it had happened the place was lost. There was no returning, that place was gone. But she knew the state existed and was what she wanted; she knew what she was aiming for.

She kept Stuart at arm's length. When he started to walk home with her at the end of school she shook her head and didn't reply to any of the notes he sent her asking her to meet him. Stuart returned to watching from a distance. Finally she found a letter he had arranged for Sandra to slip into her satchel.

'Dear Frances,' it said, 'I've been thinking about you such a lot. I've got mocks coming up and I can't concentrate on my revision. You don't understand how much you mean to me and how I miss being with you. I saw an old film on the television the other day about a man who sees a young girl skating on a frozen lake, all alone. He falls in love with her, but she was dead, just a ghost that haunted the place. But he can't stop loving her anyway, even though he knows she doesn't exist. It was a silly, romantic film, but I kept thinking of you and I found I was crying at the end. I'd rather you didn't tell that to anyone, but what I feel about you is *serious*. I can't help it. It's not just an infatuation and I won't get over it. If you go on refusing to see me I'll be like the man in the film, I'll just go on loving your ghost. Please let me be your friend. I won't do anything you don't want. We could just walk home from school or talk in the playground. Just talk to me. Please. Yours sincerely, Stuart.'

Frances hardly read the letter. She skimmed across the lines not wanting to take in the words. She thought it was silly, he was silly. But there was something that frightened her about Stuart. His persistence, his certainty, were different from the way the other boys were, the ones who claimed broken hearts to Sandra. They all got over it and were off with someone else within days or weeks. There was something about Stuart, not his words exactly, that sounded as though he meant it, and that he really wouldn't go away.

Stuart's conviction was convincing, but it scared her more than it flattered. If she was breaking his heart, she didn't want to know about it. She had liked the look of desire in his eyes, years ago, but that was when she thought that she could remain unimplicated in it. Now, it was something she didn't want to think about.

Adolescent though she was, Frances postponed any real interest in sexual matters. She had none of the normal four-teen year old's obsession with the body, either her own or the bodies of others. She hardly noticed her own physical development. The premature experiment with Stuart had been enough, and the strange night with her mother, still undefined, pushed away, too much. The whole business was best forgotten. She had put it out of her mind and certainly made no link with what had happened then and the sexual talk she heard from her classmates at school. In spite of her early forwardness, she simply could not see what all the fuss was about. A curtain of sexual innocence had fallen about her in spite of the fact that those around her were tearing away the veils with all the energy that puberty could summon.

At break-time, when it was Frances and Sandra's turn with the dog-eared, limp copy of *Lady Chatterley's Lover* that was being passed around the class, she read the marked passages without minding that she hadn't the faintest idea what they described. Sandra was much more experienced and offered an interpretation for the more obscure bits.

'Oh,' said Frances. 'I see. Is that usual?'

'No, of course not. It's really dirty doing that. Normally . . .'

Frances somehow stopped listening. Sandra's words meandered past her as if she were listening to Miss Hardi-ment explaining Ancient Egyptian irrigation methods. *Fuck-ing*, for Frances, was still a word of power, the sound of anger and energy; it barely crossed her mind to connect it with the activity it defined.

Frances's twin goals of oblivion and caring about nothing fitted neatly together to provide a framework and a method of proceeding with her life. It affected those around her too.

For Sandra there was the distress of having to say no to Frances, whose fury was less frightening than the further contempt of her parents. For Stuart there was the agony of having to say yes and violating his own judgement and character. Frances was single-minded, she wanted accomplices, but would do without them – would probably do worse without them just to show how much she didn't care. Stuart was too frightened for her to say no. He was a lover, not the stuff that refusers were made of. Frances and Stuart pursued a career of wrong-doing for precisely opposite reasons.

On Saturdays they spent the day in town together. First a ride on the Underground: no ticket at the beginning of the journey, underpaying at the other end.

'We got on at the last stop.'

They had got on five stops before. A minor misdemeanour, but only an initial warm-up for the rest of the day's activities. Stuart dreaded even this, though. He feared the humiliation of being caught, the embarrassment of being found out. Every time they went through the barrier and Frances held out the money, swinging her long red hair and laughing at a joke he hadn't told her, he felt sick with the pointless risk they were taking. And things got much worse as the day progressed.

He had fought her for days before agreeing; argued, refused, explained, begged; but Frances wanted petty larceny as badly as she had wanted ether, and Stuart wanted her just as much. There was no other way of being with her. He could only be her friend if he would be her partner in crime. He had no choice. Every Friday night he sat in his room wondering if this would be the last sensible day of his life. All the work he had put in, his prospective career, his mother's sacrificed life and health, all gone, for Frances's flirtation with the thrill of almost, nearly, perhaps tomorrow, ruining her life – and as it happened, just in passing, his too.

From the Underground they headed for one of the gloomy new coffee bars in Soho. Glass cups, frothy cappuccinos made with the maximum of noise on gurgling, sputtering machines, and low tables with spindly legs.

'OK, let's go,' Frances would say after an hour or so,

and Stuart's heart would stop again and Frances made an unhurried exit, leaving the bill unpaid and, to Stuart's eyes, spotlighted on the table. He thanked God every time that the current mood decreed not only black polo-necked sweaters, aching saxophone solos, and novels that discoursed on the hopelessness of everything, but also the lowest-wattage bulbs in the light fittings.

'For God's sake,' Frances would turn on him angrily when they were in the street. 'Don't hunch your shoulders like that. You might as well wear a sign saying, "I'm a thief, please catch me." '

Sometimes, just for his heart's sake, if Frances was far enough ahead of him, he'd turn quickly and put some money on the table, but it rarely took the edge off his terror because he was almost more frightened of Frances seeing him than of being caught leaving without paying.

Then there was the long, dreadful trip along Oxford Street, on and off buses, ticketless, of course, and in and out of stores, a small raiding party taking whatever came to hand. Frances made a point of making herself as conspicuous as possible, she said, on the grounds that no thief would draw attention to themselves like that, so no one would think they were. But Stuart knew that her chiming laughter, the little song and dance she performed every now and again, the loud contemptuous comments on the trivial purchases of other shoppers, were designed to raise the stakes. The risk of stealing wasn't great enough, the chances of getting away with it too high.

Her favourite exploit was stealing from Foyle's. She marched around the islands of stacked books picking one or two from each.

'Mmm, this looks interesting. We'll have that.' Or, 'Just the kind of rubbish Auntie Enid would like. She's never had any taste.' This last especially if someone had just chosen the book after a long examination of the front and back covers. She added each volume to the tower that Stuart carried in his arms. Sometimes, by the end of the excursion, he held fifteen or twenty books cradled in his forearms, steadying the pile with his chin. She only stopped when he was in danger of not being able to see.

'Right, that'll do,' she'd say, and then turn around and march firmly towards the door. Stuart staggered after her, like a rich woman's chauffeur laden with the day's purchases. And they would leave, Frances holding the door open for him. No one ever stopped them.

'Why should they care? Everyone knows they're underpaid students. What do they care if we walk out with a shopful of books? Anyway, *no one* would just wander out with so many books like that, it would be too obvious.'

Stuart's only comfort, as he tottered down the street, was that he was too busy not dropping his load to worry if anyone was chasing after them. The day finished with Frances distributing books to passers-by on the street. There were too many to carry home, along with the other booty.

'Do you want a book?' she'd ask anyone who caught her eye, young or old, delighted or horrified at being approached on the open street and *given* something. 'You look like a reader. We've got all these spare ones. No, you'd be doing us a favour. We've got far too many and not enough bookshelves.'

She considered the possibility of selling them back to Foyle's secondhand department, but Stuart put his foot down; the secondhand department was on a floor above the new books section.

'I am not walking back through that shop with a load of books I've just stolen. It's all I can do to walk out of it.'

Frances gave up the idea reluctantly.

'Anyway,' she added after a moment's thought, 'we don't want to actually make money. It would spoil the fun.'

'It's not fun. I've got my A levels next term. I should be at home working, not dragging around playing silly games with you.'

Frances waved her hand airily.

'Oh, you'll pass. You'll pass, and go to university and spend the rest of your life as a dreary mechanical engineer, whatever that is. These Saturdays are probably the last risk you'll ever take in your life. You'll have a nice job, and a fat wife, and two boring children, and then one day you'll be old and die. You'll look back on our Saturdays and think, that was living.'

Stuart's secret terror was that she was right. He didn't mind about the boring job, wife and kids. He minded that, however boring and satisfying they were, he would never get Frances out of his heart; that he would indeed get old and die, but that even at the moment of his death he would ache for this aggravating, unloving, little girl. Sometimes he wished he would die soon, so as not to have to go through that terrible moment of dying and longing at the end of his life. He dreaded death and Frances coming together.

'Supposing I married *you*?' he asked.

Frances made a face, as if she'd found something nasty in a pot of jam.

'Ugh. Married? I'm not going to marry anyone. Honestly, Stuart, don't be silly. And don't start talking about love and stuff, it makes me sick.'

Love and stuff made Sandra sick too.

In spite of Sandra's refusal to join in Frances's quest for oblivion or disaster, they remained friends. Frances needed a righteous witness to tell it all to. Sandra voiced all the fears that Frances could experience only as excitement.

'What will they do to you, if they catch you?'

'Borstal, I suppose. They can't put me in prison.'

'But you'd be arrested. Everyone would know. What about your parents, and everyone at school?'

A smile slipped out of Frances.

'Who cares?'

'Aren't you scared?'

The smile set hard to match the eyes, all the muscles of her face tightened into defiance to confirm the simple accuracy of her words.

'I don't care.'

Sandra shook her head.

'It must be terrible in Borstal. You'd be a criminal. What

about school? Exams, university? What would happen to you? What would your life become?'

'It'd still be my life, wouldn't it? It's always going to be my life, whatever happens. Unless I'm dead.'

Sandra didn't know what she meant by that, but it made her feel frightened, perhaps for herself as much as Frances. She didn't want to pursue the subject.

'Michael and I went all the way last night. I told Mummy I was round at your place.'

'Did you? What was it like? I thought you weren't going to do that. You're not such a goody-goody yourself, are you?'

'I didn't want to. I don't know. It just happened. You won't tell anyone, will you?'

There was rising panic in her voice.

'I really don't want to do anything wrong. Supposing they find out? I've been so frightened about the exams. How am I going to get the kind of marks I've been getting for my essays? You know I'm going to fail. They'll know I've been cheating.'

'What's that got to do with going all the way with Michael?'

'I don't know. Nothing. But I liked him being so nice to me and telling me . . . things . . . about how much he wanted me . . . and then it just sort of happened. The exams didn't seem so important for a little while. But now I'm worried about the exams *and* people finding out what I've done with Michael.'

'To say nothing of being pregnant.'

'Ssh . . . don't!' Sandra's voice dropped to an agonized whisper, as if the words themselves carried the danger of impregnation. 'It'll be all right. I know it'll be all right.' Sandra's head shook away the danger as she spoke. But it wouldn't quite disappear. 'God,' she covered her mouth with a cupped hand. 'What would I do? What would happen?'

Frances stared at her, feeling that, if ever a person needed a face like Audrey Hepburn with well-developed breasts thrown in, it wasn't Sandra. It wasn't that being beautiful and getting a double first was an impossible combination but that everything in Sandra strained towards the sensual. It was as if she were inhabited with the spirit of an houri who was devoted to the pleasures of the flesh and determined to relive those pleasures through the body of Sandra. Sandra wanted A's; her body wanted to make its mark on the world of desire. She couldn't move or, if it came to that, sit still, without seeming to offer herself. All her life she had struggled to win from her parents the love and admiration that her body could get from anyone else without trying. The look she saw in other eyes was not ever exactly satisfactory, but it began to seem close enough for comfort. And comfort had begun to seem as close as she would ever get to what she wanted.

'Oh, it'll be all right,' Frances said firmly. 'You can't get pregnant the very first time.'

Sandra looked up hopefully.

'Why not?' she asked, impatient for the relief of Frances's new information.

'Well . . . you just *can't*. It wouldn't be fair, would it?'

The two girls looked at each other blankly for a second and then turned their eyes to the floor.

'Well, it wouldn't, would it?' Frances repeated, and they both hoped that fate could hear her.

It wasn't difficult for Sandra's parents to find someone to do the abortion. They had the money and her mother had an understanding gynaecologist. The school was informed that Sandra had glandular fever and that she wouldn't be returning. By the time she had recovered she would be old enough to leave school and it had been decided that she should do a secretarial course.

Frances called several times, but Sandra's mother always answered the phone and said she wasn't available. There was a bitter edge to her voice that told Frances she knew about the essays.

Sandra managed to call Frances before she went away.

'They're sending me to a secretarial college. It's up in Scotland, I'm going to stay with my aunt. They said there's no point in my taking exams. I'm not university material.

Daddy says I'll have to be a secretary and hope for the best. He said at least I won't have to be a shop assistant, I can be grateful to my background for that.'

'What about the – you know, the operation?'

'Nobody talks about it. No one's mentioned it since I had it, except that my aunt's been told to keep me in at night and I have to be able to account for every minute of my time. My parents just said I'd disgraced them. No one talks to me about anything except to make plans for me leaving.' She was crying now. 'I hate my aunt. But I suppose there's nothing else to do. If I was like you, I'd run away.'

'I haven't run away. Where would you go?'

'I mean I wouldn't care, so it would be like running away. But I'll always care that I'm not good enough.'

'Not good enough for what?'

'For them. There's nothing I can do now that'll make anything right. It's like you said, I'll have to be me for as long as I live, and being me's no good. The best I can do is marry someone they approve of, but it'll be him they approve of, never me. It's hopeless.'

'Then why not do what you want?'

'Because there isn't anything I want except to be clever enough for them and I can't do that.'

'Well, write to me.'

'No, I don't think I will. Thinking about you getting on with your life will make me feel awful. I'm so jealous of you, the way you don't mind about things.'

Frances closed her eyes after they had stopped talking, and tried to get down into her secret place. She was still shut out.

'Funny, isn't it?' Stuart said.

They were sitting on the grass in the square near Frances's house.

'What's funny?'

'That you go around trying so hard to get caught and put away, and Sandra who cares so much about not getting into trouble ends up exiled in Scotland with her life in ruins.'

'I'm *not* trying to get caught. I'm not doing anything.'

'Still,' Stuart didn't bother to argue, 'everything Sandra minds about is wrecked. I've got a feeling that, no matter how hard you try, you're going to survive and be successful while the rest of us just fade away.'

Frances flashed a look of venom at him.

'It's not my fault.'

'No, that's the point. That's what's so funny. Things don't seem to work out the way anyone wants them to. I'll probably end up in prison, or mad, like some deranged poet, for love of you. Sandra will marry some rich bastard to please her parents, have kids to please her parents and her husband, and end up despised by all of them. And you – you'll become rich and famous and successful.'

'I don't want to be rich and famous and successful.'

'No, that's what I mean.'

'I think you should stop reading all those books by Sartre and Kerouac and people. You're beginning to sound like the bits you've read out to me. Electrical engineers shouldn't think too much, I shouldn't think.'

'Mechanical.'

'What?'

'Mechanical. I'm going to be a mechanical engineer. You're right, though, about thinking. That's what unhappiness does to you. It makes you think when you should be memorizing formulae.'

'It's not my fault you're unhappy,' Frances insisted.

'It is your fault. But it doesn't matter. I expect I'd have found some other excuse for reading Sartre if I hadn't met you.'

'Exactly, I'm just an excuse.'

Stuart didn't answer.

'Would you be happy if I let you do it to me?' Frances looked at him as if she were challenging him to a duel. Stuart took the stab of danger in his solar plexus. Frances had a new route to disaster lined up. Ether and theft hadn't got her where she wanted to be, so sex was on the agenda. Look what it had done for Sandra, after all. He kept his face immobile.

'No, I don't think it would make me happy.'

120

'Oh, so you don't want to, then?'

Stuart had a sense of a circle closing in around him.

'I do want to. I don't think it will make me happy, that's all.'

'That's nice. I thought it was what you were after all these years.'

'You're not old enough to know what I'm after. Come to that, I don't think I am either.'

'Well, then, I'm not old enough to do it with you,' Frances snapped.

'No, you never have been. Let's not talk about it.' Stuart stood up and began to walk to the gate in the railings. 'I'm going home. I've got some shopping to do for my mother and about three days' revision to catch up on.'

Frances ran to get level with him.

'Will you miss me when you go to university next year?'

'I'm trying for London.'

'Oh, why? I thought you wanted to go to Cambridge.'

He glanced at her and looked away again.

'You know why.'

'You'll probably meet some girl at university and forget all about me.'

'Shut up, Frances. I've had enough.'

Frances was quiet for a moment.

'Do you want to, then?'

'What?' The patience was leaking away. Stuart feared the misery that would replace it.

'Do it with me? I know where we could do it. There's this room under the back stairs in my block of flats. It's where the cleaners have their tea. It's supposed to be locked but they don't bother. You could meet me there this evening.'

Stuart stopped and peered at her through his glasses. For a moment his mild, boy's face looked almost haggard. Schoolwork, exams, a new life in prospect, an over-anxious mother to please; his face was filled with the stress and tensions of his eighteen years, a normal, heavy load, but overfilled too with pains that didn't belong on such a youthful face and that time wouldn't take care of.

'I'm busy this evening,' he said, trying to look determined.

Frances shrugged.

'OK. Forget it, then.'

He sighed inevitability.

'All right. I'll work late. But I have to get the shopping. I'll come about seven.'

Frances grinned at him and shook out her hair. A few blades of grass drifted on to the tarmac path.

'I hope you know how to stop people getting pregnant,' she called after him as he walked away from her in the direction of his shopping list.

Frances sat on the floor and shook her hair free from the elastic band. Stuart extended his hands, intending to run his spread fingers between the thick, burned-red strands. Frances flicked her hair back behind her shoulders.

'I think you should take your glasses off,' she said. 'Can you see without them?'

'Not very well.'

'Take them off, anyway. I haven't seen you without them.'

He put them on the table by the window.

'You look quite different. As if there was less of you and you were lost somewhere and couldn't find your way.'

'Well, I can't see very well.'

He felt vulnerable without his glasses, like a victim walking towards a bully knowing he would be beaten. He wiped his hand over the bridge of his nose and across one eye, pulling the lid towards his temple. He was quite tall, fully grown, but his face still hovered between adolescence and manhood; it carried only the suggestion of the man's face it would become.

'No, put them on again. I don't like you without them. That's better. Now, let's get on with it.'

Stuart wrapped the sticky Durex in a paper handkerchief and put it in the wastepaper bin by the door.

'Don't be silly, you can't put it there. Someone'll find it.'

He took it out and put it in his jacket pocket.

'You didn't seem to enjoy it much,' he said, without looking up.

'I don't know. It was all right. I thought it would be more . . . dangerous.'

'I'm sorry.'

'The trouble is you like me too much. You're too nice to be dangerous,' Frances pondered.

'I just want to be close to you. To hold you. I love you.'

'Well, you've got no reason to. Can't you stop it?'

'I'm sorry.'

Stuart was depressed. Frances's notion of sex was no more what Stuart wanted than stealing had been. The distance he longed to cross remained undiminished. It had been an excursion into loneliness that had nothing to do with getting closer to Frances. It was the fourth time he'd made love to a girl and not different from the other three; an act of release but empty compared to his solitary acts of love with the Frances he called up from the overflowing place in his heart. Hundreds of times he had made her come to him, conjuring her into a misty existence and slowly, slowly allowed the momentum of passion to build. He surrounded himself with her, making her substance flow around him, and letting the ache grow gently, allowing it to concentrate into an unsupportable need. He had the smooth red hair float around him and his hands peeling away her clothes as if they were layers of skin. She murmured in a voice he had never heard, using words he didn't recognize, and explained to him what he never afterwards really understood: why he needed her. She became the shape of something he had known all his life that until then had had no shape, and been no more than a vacant space.

Frances was disappointed too. It hadn't felt like a step along the rattling road to catastrophe. Stuart was right; she didn't get caught, or trapped in oblivion. Life simply went on, no matter what she did, in the way she was terrified it would. It was almost as if her capacity not to care inoculated her from disaster. It was very frustrating. Nothing seemed to destroy her, and nothing made Stuart go away. She felt his presence as a danger, as the first sign of everything going on for ever. If he would walk away from her, at least, she felt that something would have been achieved. She knew it was necessary to be isolated, to have no one and nowhere to fall back on. But Stuart loved her. He would be there to pick her up whatever she did. She was enraged. She didn't want to be tangled in someone's love. She didn't want to be cared about. She didn't want the burden of his caring. He would spoil everything by taking care of her and leading her gently and lovingly towards all those moments of misery. All the time he was there, saying, use me, don't be completely alone, rely on me. She hated him because he made her less brave than she had to be. Instead of flinging herself at disaster, she edged towards it with Stuart always by her side, offering to show her the way back.

Dancing was the only thing that gave Frances pleasure at this time. The private lessons had stopped, of course; Ivy was too distracted with her own private tragedy to concern herself with ensuring Frances's future as a lady. The only appearances that remained were those that Frances kept up and they were more internal than the wearing of white gloves and playing the piano with distinction. But dancing classes were available once a week after school and Frances had attended them regularly. Dancing made sense. It was solitary, difficult and essentially pointless. It wasn't the dancing so much as the floor and barre exercises that Frances liked. She enjoyed giving her body instructions that it had to obey. She replaced the loss of her internal space with muscle and sinew, building herself an image of a solid interior that denied and made impossible the cavernous space she could no longer reach. It was the only thing she put any real effort into, and during the week, between the classes themselves, she worked in the gym at lunch-break to maintain and increase the control.

Her teacher was impressed, and so was the man from the

dance company that she brought in one day to look at Frances work.

'Have you thought of dance as a career? I think you've got the talent and the will.'

Frances stared hard at him.

'I'm sure I could arrange a scholarship for you to train with us. Or are you committed to exams?'

Frances shook her head slowly.

'Could I start next year?' she asked.

'Yes, if you get through the audition. Would you like to?'

'And the scholarship. Would it be enough to live on? I mean, could I live in digs? You know, leave home?'

The man from the dance company nodded.

'You'd have to have your parents' permission, of course. You'd still only be sixteen. Do you think they'd agree?'

Frances bent down to rub her calf muscle.

'Yes, I think so. I don't think that'll be a problem.'

'Good, then I'll arrange the audition. I think you may have a bright future.'

Frances smiled down the new escape route that life, in one of its small convulsions, had unexpectedly provided.

– So Stuart was right. Your mother was to become successful and famous.

– There was a danger of that. But don't forget I said the story had a sad ending.

– Yes, I remember, the mother dies and the child dies. It's a little hard to credit with you as narrator.

– It's only a matter of waiting. That's what I'm here for, taking up crib space – to wait for the end. There are those who resent it, who feel that an orphaned anhydranencephalic would be better despatched quickly than left to some opportunistic infection. They feed me enough to prevent starvation, but they won't, as they say, be officious about keeping me alive when a passing virus takes up residence. It's morally flabby, of course, but what can I do about human equivocation? I'm hardly in a position to express my opinion and, if I could, who would take it seriously? Someone would be sure to point out that I'm below the age of consent.

– But, if you could, you would choose oblivion?

– It doesn't matter. There's no pain either way.

– None?

– None. How could there be? And this way I get to finish my mother's story.

– More or less.

– Yes, more or less.

– Don't you fear the end?

– Which end, mine or the story's?

– Doesn't it amount to the same thing?

– I suppose you're right. Either way there's silence. What can there be to fear about silence?

– Did Frances fear death?

– No, you'll see. What she feared was life.

126

– But she became a dancer. Wasn't that a very positive thing to do for someone like her?

– All the time, all through her time, she was after the lessening of herself. Every refusal, every act was a stripping away. Now, she thought each time, there's nothing left. It felt like that, but she never quite managed to make herself disappear. She never got thin enough to squeeze back into her special place.

– But why dancing?

– I don't know. It focused everything down to a pin-point. There was only body, movement and space. It was another route to oblivion. Once, after she had spooned a soft supper between my unresponsive lips, she picked me up in her arms and began to spin a slow waltz around the kitchen table. 'This is dancing, Nony,' she hummed. 'You'll never dance and you'll never be wicked.' Naturally I couldn't hear her words or feel the cool air brush against my skin as we whirled, but I *heard* and *felt* in my way. But even perceiving her thoughts as directly as I did, it wasn't clear whether she was pitying or congratulating me. Dancing and wickedness were much the same thing to my mother.

– She made no headway with wickedness?

– It didn't seem to change anything, did it? She made her way to the boiler-house after her disappointment with Stuart, and made herself available. You know, hands up sweaters, hands on cocks. The full thrust every now and again. Nothing happened. No pregnancy, no expulsion. She didn't even get herself a name as the school slag. There was something about her manner that stopped that from happening. She was a disastrous failure at disaster.

– So she danced instead?

– Think of the endless opportunities for looking in mirrors that a dancing career offers. If she couldn't manage oblivion, she could at least keep checking on her posture. Why don't I just go on with the story? I may start sneezing any moment.

– What if you finish too soon? What if there turns out to be more time than you thought? Do you have another story to fill in with?

– What other story could I have?

– I only ask because I have my future to consider too. I wonder what my existence would be like without anything to listen to.

– You'll have to listen to the silence, I suppose, if I finish too soon. But don't worry, it won't be for long, there's no prognosis. Time will take care of both of us.

– A comforting thought, but I've only got your word for it. Come to think of it, I've only got your word for anything. It's a very one-sided view of the universe.

– It's the only game in town. You're in no position to ask for a second opinion. Take my universe or leave it.

– Where would I go? I don't have any qualifications for another universe. Maybe I'll strike out on my own. A willing ear for hire. Have ear, will travel. Could you give me a reference?

– I'm afraid your fate is sealed. When I go, you go too. Think of the two of us as an exploding star in some far-off galaxy. No one will ever know we've been or gone. There's something magnificent about extinction, don't you think?

– Not if no one ever knew of our existence in the first place.

– You don't like the idea of being an undiscovered secret?

– Not much. I'd prefer a little recognition. The odd talk-show; an interview or two; a commemorative medal struck in appreciation of my selfless service to anhydranencephalics.

– It's just as well that time's running out. You're beginning to get out of hand.

– You're right, there's probably nothing more unsatisfying than a disembodied ego. I'm just an itch with nothing to scratch. Go on, then, let's hear how time took care of Frances.

– Now you're being a sensible non-being.

NINETEEN SIXTY TWO was the coldest winter this century, but Frances had her *pliés* to keep her warm. There was nothing but dancing for the next four years. She flung herself into it as if it were driftwood and she afloat in an empty sea. It was all there was, not a direction but an absence of drowning.

Every morning she arrived at the school by eight for an hour's warm-up before her first class, wrapped against the cold in one of Stuart's thick turtle-neck jumpers and an oversized duffel coat from an army surplus store. Apart from the compulsory classes, she attended several others, including public evening classes. She never got home before nine in the evening. Stuart would be waiting for her with a meal.

'You've got to eat properly. You're working much too hard. You don't get enough rest,' he worried as he put a large plate of steaming, calorific spaghetti in front of her. 'You're getting terribly thin.' Frances hunched over the plate, turning her fork aimlessly in the centre of the tangled strands. 'Did you eat lunch?'

Frances rested her head in the hand that was not toying with the spaghetti.

'I don't need lunch when I've got this mountain of food to get through in the evening. I'm not losing weight, I'm exchanging fatty tissue for muscle. It makes me look different.'

'You weren't exactly fat to start with.'

'I have to get the machine right. Ze bodee,' she intoned, 'is ze macheen of God. Ve must use eet like a prayeur, but ve must get ze verds r-r-right. Ze muscles are ze verds of our prayeur, each vun must be purrfect for eets position in ze scheme of theengs.'

'Christ, what a load of rubbish.'

Frances pushed her plate away.

'Yes. But the fact is I can't do what I have to do unless the muscles are in the right condition.'

'You've still got to eat. There's more going on in the world than your dance classes.'

'I don't care.'

'You should care.'

Frances got that dangerous look on her face that finished the conversation.

'I . . . don't . . . care.'

Stuart cleared the table. Frances got up.

'I'm going to practise.' She floated off into her room where Stuart had fixed a rail for her barre exercises.

Stuart took the small pile of books he'd set aside on the sofa while Frances ate, and banged them angrily on the table. He'd changed in the last year, or perhaps allowed a part of himself to grow like his hair, which flopped down over his forehead, bothering his eyes. The old spectacles had been replaced with heavier, squarer ones with thick black rims. His face remained boyish, a slight chip on his front tooth retained his air of adolescence, but his grey eyes, though still lost-looking, had a darker, worried aspect. He dressed now in thick, high-necked fisherman's sweaters and loose jeans. There had always been a serious, vaguely troubled look about him, but now his appearance and the anxiety that flickered behind the lenses of his glasses seemed weightier, less the passing shyness of adolescence, but something fundamental of his own, as though he had excavated his shadowy places and found the darkness to be the very substance of himself.

He had no trouble pursuing his engineering degree but found it, and the career he should have been planning, mattered much less than the discoveries he had been making in books that were not part of the course reading-list.

The books on the table, along with scraps of paper covered with notes, were not engineering texts. Camus's *The Myth of Sisyphus* and Laing's *The Divided Self* lay open in front of him. *Capital* waited, closed, for his attention along with

Engels's *The Origins of the Family* and various volumes of critical comment on Marxist theory. He had divided his reading into two separate piles, but both occupied space on the table. He hadn't finally decided what name to give the nagging discontent that drew him inconclusively to both visions of the world.

He spent his evenings in dark basements, thick with smoke, sharp with the wafting scent of burning weed, listening to the languishing trumpets and melancholic saxophones of jazz groups disturbing familiar tunes into a common language of despondency. The long solos strung out notes like a search-beam lighting up a route to nowhere, making a bright corridor in the blackness that proved only that the blackness went on interminably, far beyond the limits of yearning.

In the pauses between the sets he talked with friends who were strangers before their accidental meeting that evening in the club and would be strangers the next morning even if the remainder of the night was spent in their bed. They discussed Kerouac and Burroughs, Camus and Kafka, Dostoevsky and Hardy, and the next morning parted, the grey light of dawn confirming the isolation that had been the subject of their discourse. Girls turned gratefully to the wall as the sound of the door closing assured them of a few more hours sleep. Men said, 'Yeah, man, catch you soon,' and scratched their balls in preparation for the day's rest. Stuart walked home, his grandiose solitude, that last night had been a match for Raskolnikov and Jude, diminished in the damp, ordinary morning to look no more than lonely, sad, shy – small. No different, probably, from what Raskolnikov or Jude would have felt if fiction hadn't made it all much grander. Still, by evening the music was inflating the pain again and making it seem worthwhile.

But he hadn't dropped out. He didn't get home and crawl into bed to prepare himself for the coming night of moody despair. He washed and changed and took himself off to college for a day bent over textbooks in the library. He accepted grimly that he had to complete his course and that when he had he would have to take a job. He owed it to his mother to accept the prize of a career with prospects that they

131

had both worked so hard for. But he wouldn't be engaged in the task, wherever he was; he knew that. The official studying and the coming career were like housekeeping; a necessary nuisance. He would do what had to be done to succeed at the engineering degree, and do it efficiently, not with success in mind, but so that it would take as little time as possible away from his real interests, the politics and philosophy and the background music.

And Frances. She remained the source of pain, like a natural spring in the earth that bubbled away unconcerned. All the other thoughts seemed to arise from the turbulent place in him that contained Frances, the discontents, the doubts, the anger at a world, not of his making, but unfathomable, troubling.

When she told him of her plans he tried to persuade her that it was foolish to waste her grant renting a room, when she could stay with him in his small flat, and moved his bed into the living-room so that Frances could have a room of her own. She refused at first and shared a flat with several other girls from her dance course. It wasn't long before she arrived at his door with her suitcase, looking sullen, defeated by the camaraderie of girls together.

'You'll leave me alone, won't you?' she had demanded angrily, before she crossed the threshold.

'In what way?' he asked, brushing his hair back away from his eyes.

'In every way.'

But she had let him put up the railing in her room and keep the larder stocked.

Frances sat on the sprung floorboards of the empty practice studio and checked her position in the mirror that covered the wall facing her. She clasped the inside of each thigh and pushed outwards, gaining a few inches of extra width for the angle between her legs, then braced her palms on the floor in front of her to lift herself slightly and press her pelvis towards the mirror, widening her legs still further. She checked her reflection. Her back, neck and head ran in a single straight line of controlled tension from floor to the top of her skull. Her head, balanced on a single column of carefully built support, was high and centred, her shoulders dropped away easily and naturally to either side of her spine. The tight black leotard emphasized the structure of her torso: a concave abdomen, hard-walled with muscle, and above it the undulations of her ribs and flattened breasts. Her body was a working summary of the twin qualities of strength and structure required by the demands of dance. She examined the contrast of her barely fleshed skeleton and the precise swelling of carefully developed muscle groups: calf, thigh, shoulders. The essential image of the dancer reflected back at her satisfactorily; not her, but a form designed to fulfil a particular function. A wide band of material controlled her russet hair, scraped back and twisted tightly into a bun at the nape of her neck, making her face conform, expressionless, sharply contoured, to the accepted notion of the dancer.

When she was satisfied with what she saw she turned the upper part of her torso to the right, let her chest drop forward on to her thigh and held either side of her ankle with each hand, elbows bent, stretching herself carefully. She held the position, her forehead on her knee, her spine reaching, elongating, trying for an impossible extension towards her flexed foot.

'. . . two, three, four, five, six, seven . . .' she counted off silently. She heard the door of the practice room open and close. On 'eight' she lifted herself back to centre and saw Stuart's reflection watching her in the mirror.

'What are you doing here?' she asked and then dropped forward so that she lay flat, folded in half, in the space between her legs, her arms extending towards the mirror.

'I'm going to a demonstration at Trafalgar Square. I thought you might like to come.'

'You mustn't wear shoes in here. I can't go anywhere until I've finished practising. Anyway, why would I want to go to a demonstration? What about?' She kept her position but lifted her chin so that she could look at Stuart in the glass.

Stuart stared sternly at her through the mirror, clutching a pile of papers against his student scarf. 'Frances, even you must have noticed that there's a crisis going on.'

'The Cuban thing? . . . seven . . . eight.' She straightened her back and then bent down to the left. 'I don't want to go to a meeting. I haven't finished here. What for, anyway? What's it supposed to do?'

'The fucking world's about to blow up and all you can do is jerk about in front of a mirror getting your muscles right. What's more important, the world on the brink of atomic war or the condition of your body?'

'. . . six . . . seven . . . eight. The condition of my body.' Up again to centre, then back down to the right. 'What will me and my muscles do if the world doesn't blow up?'

'You can't spend your life being a doll, staring at yourself in the mirror. You've got a mind as well as a body. You can't just reject it. It's narcissistic, dancing, it's irrelevant.'

'Go away. Go to your meeting.' She raised one arm over her head, still bent sideways, and pulled towards the right wall. 'You're making me lose count . . . four . . . five . . . six . . . seven . . .'

Stuart stood and watched her work, impressed, in spite of his disapproval, by the extraordinary suppleness of her movements and the control that was at the centre of it. He squatted down beside her.

'Look, I've got to go. Come with me. Please.'

'Well, go then. I'll see you later. The bomb's not going off this evening, is it? Will the fish and chip shop be open?'

'I'll get some on the way back. Haven't you eaten anything today?'

He wanted to stay and watch her. He wondered why he had come; there wasn't the slightest chance that she would go to the demo with him. He wanted her to go to the meeting like he wanted them to live together properly, as lovers. He wanted her to read his books and stroke his hair absentmindedly as she turned a page. But he was beginning to understand that if she did those things, and made the pain in him go away, he would miss it, that through habit or inclination the pain was the most important thing in his life. It seemed to him sometimes to be his only unique quality. If he loved Frances, and he did, it was because she nurtured his hopelessness and kept the fire of his pain stoked. And what else was there that proved to him that he was alive?

I hate him, she thought when he had gone, why doesn't he leave me alone?

Stuart's offer of a room in his flat had made her heart sink. She knew, even as she moved in with her fellow students, that she would end up on his doorstep. She didn't want to gossip and giggle with them, and she had no interest in the endless dance chat. She didn't want to talk about it, she just wanted to do it and be left alone. On a small grant, Stuart was the only option. It had, as he said, made sense. But she was still angry. She wished he wasn't there for her all the time, that his continual presence in her life wasn't so practically useful. He tried to keep his distance, but she felt his worry and concern, and lately there was a new pressure from his need to have her understand the thoughts that had seeped out of his books and whirled uncomfortably around his head. She didn't want to know, she didn't want to understand. He wanted her to join him. She couldn't and wouldn't. But there was nowhere else to go, that she could see. And it was true that he looked after everything. He made sure that she was fed and warm and didn't have to worry about anything except her practice. He made life easier. She seethed with resentment at how hard he made it for her to leave. His being there took care of so much that she didn't want to have to deal with. And leaving would have been so positive an act of independence; a statement about herself that she had no desire to make.

She had taken the cocoon he offered as a way of continuing to refuse to own her life. It was some comfort that Stuart disliked what she was doing. Dancing was narcissistic, a concentration on the machine, a rejection of mind. Yes, it was, and what a stroke of luck that she had found it. And if tomorrow the world was going to come to an end because of events thousands of miles away, she didn't care at all. It was all the same to her. She would continue to exercise in front of the mirror. She straightened her back slowly and began to do waist bends.

There was no doubt at the end of three years that Frances would gain a place in the Company. Her single-mindedness had ensured it. She had developed her technique, concentration and physique to a point where it was unthinkable that she should do anything else.

A few days before the final selection audition Frances received a phone call from her father.

'It's your mother. She's had an accident,' he told her in a clipped voice. She had hardly seen either of them since she began her course. Gerald paused for a moment, waiting for her to ask what had happened. The silence remained unbroken, until he continued.

'Walked in front of a car just outside the flats. Drunk. Didn't know what she was doing.'

Frances still waited. More than anything she waited to find a response to the news; some reaction that could be conveyed down the telephone line. She found nothing.

'She's in a coma. The doctors don't think she'll come out of it.'

Frances found a question.

'What hospital is she in?'

Gerald told her the name of the hospital and the ward.

'I've been to see her. There's nothing to be done, they said.' His voice was gruff, embarrassed by having to relate a drama that he wasn't entitled to feel as tragedy. 'Silly cow was drunk, as always. I'm surprised it hasn't happened before. There's nothing anyone can do. If you want to visit her, you can go any time; they don't have set visiting hours in the intensive-care unit.'

She walked to the hospital. It wasn't far from the school. She thought she could make it to the afternoon class after she had seen Ivy.

It was raining. She looked down at the glossy grey paving stones. The drops of rain splashed, fragmenting against the

136

hard surface like tiny bombs. She watched the placing of her feet, one in front of the other, a careful, deliberate tread. Frances remembered walking, not far from here, with Ivy when she was perhaps eight or nine. It had been raining then, too, and she had kept her head lowered, concentrating on the sound her shoes made on the wet pavement and noticing for the first time the mechanism of walking: heel making contact with the ground then the lowering of the rest of the foot, rolling through the length of the sole against the ground until the heel was raised and the other foot had to move forward and drop its heel against the paving stones to restore the balance. The forward movement was achieved through the attempt not to fall over, she realised. It was the first time she had been aware of walking, of how it was done. She watched each foot perform, left, right, left, right, and between each step a moment of imbalance. The rain was pouring down and it was evening, quite late, past her bedtime. Ivy had told her to put on her raincoat instead of getting ready for bed and they had left the flat. Frances had no idea why, or where they were going, but she didn't want to ask. Ivy had been drinking. Gerald hadn't come home, although the supper was waiting for him. They walked for half an hour before Frances asked what was happening.

'I'm leaving the bastard. I've had enough.'

'Where are we going?' Frances asked.

'We haven't got anywhere to go,' Ivy snapped.

Frances was terrified by the discovery that they had been walking in the rain without any direction. She had thought that they were going somewhere. Until that moment there had always been somewhere to go: home, school, the shops, always somewhere at the end of a journey. For the first time, now, it occurred to her that there might be nowhere to go, there might be just the placing of one foot in front of another without any destination. It seemed, suddenly, quite possible that the two of them could walk through the streets for ever. If there was no destination, why would it ever stop? What would happen when they got tired or hungry?

'Where are we going to sleep?' she asked, still staring down at the soaking pavement.

'We'll sleep under the arches at Charing Cross. That's what the tramps do and that's what we are, thanks to him.' Ivy's voice was loud, and triumphant with their tragedy. Frances was frightened that someone would hear.

But there was some comfort in Ivy's answer. Frances hadn't the faintest idea what the arches under Charing Cross were. Charing Cross was a bridge on the river, she knew. She imagined herself lying on the bank, surrounded by tramps, the dark water from the river lapping at her feet. The tramps, the cold and the dark worried her, but at least the arches at Charing Cross was *somewhere*.

They had walked for another hour and a half. Frances desperately wanted to be in her bed. She wanted to be warm and somewhere she knew. She began to cry.

'Stop it,' Ivy muttered, shaking Frances's sleeve. 'Blame him. He does nothing but cause misery. Stop crying.'

But she couldn't, although she tried to contain the sound.

'I want to go home,' she sobbed quietly, suddenly more frightened of the tramps than of Ivy's wrath. 'Please, can't we go home?'

Eventually they did, once the terror had been fully stoked, with Ivy blaming Frances all the way for their return.

Frances watched her feet propelling her towards the hospital where Ivy lay in a coma. She shook the old memory away and remembered her destination. She tried to think of something pleasant about Ivy, some happy memory, something that would allow her to approach the hospital bed kindly. Nothing came. There must have been moments, she knew, when the three of them were at ease together, must have been times when she was held, told stories, looked forward to an outing – something. She knew those times must have existed. But nothing came. She couldn't find anything to warm the moment when she saw her dying mother.

She arrived at the intensive-care unit chilled from the rain and her inability to find a glimmer of kindness for the woman who had given birth to her. She dreaded seeing Ivy. What was she supposed to do? She felt nothing, so what was she supposed to do? And if, when she saw her, unconscious, hooked up to machines, she was suddenly overcome with

138

sadness, what would it be for? It would be dishonest to pretend an emotion she didn't feel, and just as dishonest to feel an emotion that the situation·itself whipped up. If she was upset it would only be about death and mothers and a sense of loss, not about Ivy's death, not about her, not about Frances's loss. She felt a stubborn refusal rise from her even as the grief swelled in her throat and threatened tears. It isn't true, she told herself coldly, it isn't real. What was she grieving for? Even now she couldn't think of a single reason. The lump in her throat was physical, there was nothing that matched it deeper in herself. Nothing in herself at all but cold anger at the false, easy reaction of tears that made her feel ashamed of the hypocrisy.

'I'm very sorry,' the nurse told her. 'I'm afraid your mother died a few minutes ago. Would you like to see her?'

Frances shook her head. She felt light-headed with relief. The nurse took her elbow, steadying her.

'Come and sit down and I'll get you a cup of tea.' She was kind, and there was no judgement at Frances's refusal to look at the body. She understood how upsetting these things were.

I'm not kind, Frances told herself, lodging the thought in her mind as a permanent statement about herself. Long red hair, a fine bone structure, intelligent, and not kind. An addition to the bank of information. Not honest either. If she were honest why had she come? What for?

She looked up to see Gerald arriving through the swing doors. She stood up as he approached.

'She's dead,' Frances told him briskly.

Gerald's looks had entirely gone now. The handsome face she remembered was encased in loose, red-veined flesh, the body uncomfortably bloated. He was dingy and yellowed with time.

'Oh,' he said, pressing his lips together and lifting his jaw in acknowledgement of his daughter's words. He shifted his eyes from her face and shuffled his feet with the extreme difficulty of knowing what to say or how to respond.

'She was drunk,' he mumbled.

'Why are you here?' Frances asked, narrowing her eyes.

Gerald shuffled again.

'To see . . . her . . . your mother . . .'

Frances noticed for the first time that he held a bunch of chrysanthemums dangling, blooms down, in his fist. She wanted to laugh.

'Who are they for?'

'I brought them for her,' he said, lifting the bunch up and looking at them as though he'd never seen them before. He paused for a moment, then looked directly at his daughter as if he'd remembered who she was. 'We didn't have much of a marriage, but at the beginning it was all right. I don't know what went wrong. She drank. She drank before I met her. But I wasn't perfect. It just didn't work.' He shook his head, puzzled, wondering what he was trying to say. 'I'm sorry she's dead . . . like this . . .' He shrugged helplessly.

'You're no better at it than I am,' Frances sighed. 'I expect you're pretty relieved.'

Gerald shook his head in vehement denial.

Frances buttoned up her coat and swung her bag of dance gear over her shoulder.

'It's hard to know how to behave, isn't it, when someone you can't stand suddenly becomes a tragic death? I'm going, I've got a class to attend.'

Gerald put his hand out to stop her.

'What about your mother?' he asked in alarm.

'She's dead.'

'But what about her things? What about the funeral?'

Frances turned back and stared at Gerald, her red hair swinging with the sudden change of direction.

'I don't want anything to do with it. I don't care what you do with her things, and I won't be coming to the funeral. Bye.'

Gerald watched her disappear down the corridor and through the lift door. He looked so confused that a nurse stopped and asked him which ward he was looking for. At the sound of her voice and the sight of her pretty face he tried to stand taller, straightening his back and lifting his head. He held the chrysanthemums out towards her as if they were a passport.

'It's my wife. I've come to see my wife . . .'

140

Stuart took a job with a large engineering firm. He was expected to do well. 'A real high-flier,' he was told at his interview. He wore the suit his mother kept for him at home, and they were tolerant about the length of his hair. They liked 'a little individuality'. Stuart didn't mention his involvement with the Committee of 100 or that the book currently lying open on the living-room table was Bakunin.

Stuart's inner despair had developed beyond resignation and the dignity of lived hoplessness. He had with the aid of various texts learned to universalise his pain, to connect it to the anguish imposed by repression and deprivation all over the Western world. He no longer felt he looked out at the world through the portholes of his eyes, singular and isolated within his own consciousness. Now he found enough reason for his despair in the material world. He was flooded with relief. There was something to be done about pain that had a cause. A symptom was relieved by dealing with the underlying disease. Cure was not in suicide – he threw the existentialists, the Beats, the haunting saxophone solos, the nineteenth-century gloom-merchants to one side – but in acts of retaliation. There was an enemy.

Every night now there were meetings to plan demonstrations and actions against the forces of repression and state violence. Secret weapons establishments, chemical warfare laboratories, the army, the police, the judiciary. All these were to be exposed, to be seen by the public as repositories of power that served only their own end which was nothing more than the maintenance of the control of the many by the very few. Once the public knew the nature of the system that kept them acquiescent, they would rise against it, and take control of their own destiny.

Frances got used to coming home to a room full of conspiring young men who fell quiet at her entrance.

'It's all right,' she would say, stepping lightly over the papers and pamphlets that littered the floor, her dancer's feet dexterously avoiding the over-loaded saucers that served as ashtrays. 'I'm just passing through. Don't mind me.'

When there was a meeting, Stuart always prepared something beforehand for Frances to eat when she got home and left it in the kitchen.

'She's a dancer,' he would explain to any new member of the committee, who would nod sympathetically and return to the item under discussion. It was understood that fellow activists were not to be judged by their women who, with one or two notable exceptions, were not politically or intellectually motivated. A man might live with someone, sleep with them, feel affection even, but at best these companions were recreational; the real business of life, the commitment, was to the group and through it the destruction of the status quo. They barely raised their eyes when Frances entered the room but her complete indifference to their activities made them uncomfortably aware of her. More usually their females sat, like revolutionary geishas, cross-legged on the floor, their long hair hanging like a curtain over their lowered faces, present but not participant, except when coffee was called for. Sometimes they might act as secretary, which still kept their heads lowered with the business of taking notes, but none passed jauntily through the room, as Frances did, with her head erect, so plainly uninterested and unimpressed by the subversion being fomented in her midst.

Stuart was a quiet-looking revolutionary. His look of sincerity gave a special credibility to his new-found fervour. A calm, reserved man, who could be depended on. A comrade and an intellectual. Passion, his fellow conspirators felt, ran deeper in quiet types. There was no fire or ferocity, but he was all the more valued for that. Others might lead, and make converts with their inspired rhetoric, but Stuart provided the calm analysis, the solidity, that kept people at the daily grind of revolution. He was listened to as a mother telling a bedtime story to an over-excited child, with relief for the opportunity to quieten for the night. He was, therefore, to be forgiven for the high-stepping, sauntering girl who seemed to deem them as inconsequential as furniture.

Frances was dismissive.

'You've got your job. Now you should marry the fat, boring wife. Fat, boring comrades aren't the same thing.'

'The job's a cover. It's not what I'm really doing.'

'Well, it's just as well you've got it, because when the revolution doesn't come the money'll come in handy.'

'I'm committed to the destruction of the capitalist system,' Stuart insisted, ladling steaming porridge into Frances's bowl. She sprinkled sugar over it without enthusiasm.

'It's just a hobby. You never had a hobby, if you don't count that time on the bombsite. It's like stamp collecting or train spotting. You've got an outside interest.'

'What do you know about anything?' he yelled, partly from having burned himself on the saucepan. 'You haven't read anything, or been anywhere. You're wilfully ignorant of everything.'

'I know enough to know that knowing things doesn't help anything, and that doing things is just doing things. In the end all you lot are doing is joining in. I may be ignorant, but you're stupid.'

'There must be change. There must be people who fight for change.'

Frances sucked the porridge from the spoon and sneered.

'And there must be people who fight against change, and if either of you didn't exist neither of you could. You might as well dance; at least there are some solos to be had.'

'That's sheer bourgeois individualism.'

Frances widened her eyes in mock horror.

'I'm shameless, aren't I? Like Marie Antoinette. Grow up, Stuart, you just joined a club, that's all. I don't suppose it'll do any more harm than joining Mensa. A bit silly, but basically harmless.'

Stuart banged the cup he had just dried on to its saucer so hard that the saucer separated neatly into two parts.

'This isn't a game. It's deadly serious. There are people working for the cause, risking everything, their freedom . . . everything.'

'Are you risking your freedom?'

Stuart's eyes glistened behind his glasses.

'I've got access to documents at work. Plans . . .'

'Plans of what?'

'Installations, weapons, stuff they've got government contracts for. We can make the information public, and there's sabotage, of course.' He stopped himself. 'You mustn't breathe a word of this to anyone. It could be terribly dangerous. There's a chance we're being watched, as it is.'

'Well, it wouldn't be any fun if you weren't being watched, would it?'

Stuart hunched over in his seat and clasped his hands behind his neck.

'You're frivolous. You aren't serious,' he said, shaking his head slowly, trying to make the damning adjectives burn through his longing for her.

'And you've just noticed that? And there's you with your commitment to the overthrow of the state, deeply serious, making breakfast for me. The toast's on fire.'

He jumped up and flung the flaming toast into the sink.

'You can laugh at me, but it's the first time I've been really involved. It's like I've been an amnesiac and suddenly discovered I've got a family and a job. That I belong somewhere. Got something to do.'

Frances shrugged dismissively.

'If it's a family you want, why not get a real one?'

'Because I'll never have the one I really want.' His eyes on her rooted her to the spot. 'At least I can be useful. There are important things to do. Much more important than mere personal feelings. Or even personal security. I don't know why you're so surprised; you used to be the risk-taker, the one who had nothing to lose. You could do anything because nothing mattered. Remember?'

She had to shake herself free from his gaze.

'It wasn't the same thing, I wasn't trying to save the world. That's ridiculous. Childish. Anyway, it didn't work, did it? I didn't get what I wanted.'

'Neither did I. If I'm going to play a part in overthrowing the system, it's partly thanks to you. You might find that you've helped to save the world, in spite of yourself.'

Frances felt the rage bubbling.

'It's not my fault you're in love with me. I'm not going to take responsibility for you ending up with a life sentence for treason or terrorism, or whatever it is you're up to. It's got nothing to do with me.'

She stood up and faced him squarely over the table. Cruelty and truth demanded that the record be set straight.

'I don't love you. I don't care about you. If you went away, I'd miss the things you do for me, but I wouldn't miss you. Are you listening? I don't care about anything or anyone. I never will.'

She spoke the words clearly as if she were speaking to a foreigner. It was essential that he understood that they were the truth.

'I don't believe you,' Stuart said quietly. 'You're a human being with the same needs as everyone else. You may not love me, but it doesn't mean you won't ever care about anyone. You're afraid to care.'

Frances felt the panic of someone trying to explain to a child that a parent was dead; really dead and never coming back. It was most important that the facts were stated and believed.

'No. I'm afraid I don't care. That's the really frightening truth. It's not a story I tell about myself, but plain fact. Why can't you accept that, if I can?'

Stuart poured what was left in the teapot into his cup, concentrating on the diminishing trickle. 'If you say so.'

Frances could see that he didn't believe her, that he wasn't really listening.

Suddenly it was imperative that the secret be revealed, that the truth be acknowledged. She had kept it to herself; even, until that day in the hospital, from herself, ever since the place inside her that she went to as a child had disappeared. Down there, in the treasure-house of her self, she sat peacefully sorting through nuggets of gold and sparkling jewels; they were there and she had known, whatever happened in the world outside, how full and weighty and bright the contents were. But they had vanished, like fairy gold. The place where they were stored had become unreachable, and now she knew it hadn't ever been there, that it was a mirage of childhood. There was no content. Nothing. That was what she was.

She wanted to say to someone, 'I am a person who doesn't care, doesn't feel, doesn't love anyone or anything. That's what I am.' And to have that person answer, 'Yes, it's true there are people like that, and, yes, you are one of them.'

But she knew that no one would. They would always choose to believe that deep down, despite her statements of the truth, despite her behaviour, she cared, that she was capable of feeling. It was concealed, perhaps, barricaded behind her defensiveness, but it was there, intact, waiting for liberation. The notion comforted people, even though daily in their newspapers they read of acts and omissions that led to no other conclusion than that there were people who were devoid of feeling. When she read those reports, she recognized herself. She wanted to tell someone that. She was empty. A fact. She could walk away from anyone with a shrug. A fact. But she knew no one wanted to know what she really was. She wanted the truth about her known; she didn't want to live in the fairyland of other people's fantasies.

But telling people did no good. They didn't believe her. So she danced.

Frances rifled through her bag that she had left by the kitchen door until she found her purse.

'Here,' she said, putting a ticket on the table in front of Stuart. 'Come and see the production tomorrow night. You've never seen me perform.'

Stuart fingered the ticket.

'I can't, I've got a meeting tomorrow night.'

'Miss it. I want you to come. They won't cancel the revolution just because you've missed one meeting.'

Stuart took his seat with resignation. He was not looking forward to the next hour. The auditorium was full. Seven hundred people surrounded him waiting for the performance to begin. The Company had an international reputation, and every performance played to full houses. But it was hardly a popular art form, Stuart reminded himself. Modern ballet was a rarefied experience for the very few. And it certainly didn't interest him. It was, in fact, the first time he'd ever been to one. He liked music and he liked words, but dance of this kind was so self-absorbed, so inaccessible. He loved Frances and would have done anything she asked of him. His being at the theatre tonight felt like the old days when he had held a handkerchief soaked in ether over her nose, or carried a burden of stolen books through the street. He didn't approve but in the end he couldn't refuse her. At least dancing wasn't dangerous. Perhaps things were improving.

He glanced at his watch. Seven thirty. His meeting would have started. They had relocated it at Tom's house when he explained that his mother was sick and he'd have to go and see her. The house lights began to fade very slowly. There was a full minute of silence before the darkness was total, the stage invisible. It was another sixty seconds before the stage was suddenly illuminated with the harsh, yellow beams of six separate spotlights, each one focusing on a perfectly motionless figure surrounded by blackness and silence.

The six dancers posed like limp puppets, bent double, their arms hanging loosely to the ground, as a low electronic hum became barely audible. The sound expanded gradually into an increasingly urgent pulse that became music and wound itself and the scene on stage into life.

One by one, in turn, each figure stiffened and began to explore the empty spaces of the stage. Their movements across the dim spaces between the spotlights were sharp and jagged, tremulous with fear and suspicion; the empty distance to be traversed and the movements needed to do so posing a danger for beings wrenched out of stillness. The single figure cut a fearful route across the stage until he or she came across one of the others, who remained as they had been since the lights first came up; still and lifeless. Then the moving figure seemed to sneer with his or her body at the inert forms of the others it came across, and wove a scornful assertion of power around each of the passive bodies it confronted.

Stuart took in the intention of the piece and admired the skilled movement of the dancers without being able to find any real enthusiasm. Frances was the last to come to life. The others on the stage had each had their moment of vigour

147

before sinking back once again to their original torpor. Stuart was quite relieved that there was only one to go, and began to feel that the end was in sight. He was starting to feel hungry and looked forward to dinner with Frances who soon would have done her piece, the final repetition.

Frances looked much the same as the others on stage. She was dressed in a skintight, skin-coloured leotard that showed her lean form, and emphasized the flexure of the muscles in thigh and calf, giving away the control and strength required to maintain the flopped puppet position for so long. She hadn't moved a millimetre since the lights went up. She was differentiated from the rest only by her hair, which, although pulled back into a uniform dancer's bun, gleamed deeply and richly red under her private spotlight.

In the pause that focused attention on her immobile body Stuart found himself remembering the child on the bombsite. He waited, excited suddenly, knowing that when she lifted herself up to face the audience he would see the old expression, the impassive face surrounded by the glinting sunlit hair and the challenge in her eyes demanding that they keep their distance, daring them to move closer. It seemed to him that the entire audience held its breath, that it waited almost beyond endurance for her to come alive.

Her choreographed movements were no different from the other dancers but, as soon as she began to uncurl the lower part of her spine, she commanded a special attention. Each vertebra seemed to move separately, realigning as she straightened. Stuart and the rest of the audience were transfixed by the progression of minute internal shifts that brought her to the vertical. It was as if she had stripped away her skin to expose the mechanism of movement itself. They felt they actually saw the workings of the machine, and would have watched her spine unfolding for an eternity with rapt attention.

When she finally moved across the stage, it was with equal precision. It appeared that every movement began at, stemmed from, the slim central column of her spine, the mainspring that fired life into her limbs like small explosions from centre to periphery. She presented a force of energy in

148

a way that none of the other dancers had, but there was nothing human in her dance. Her eyes were open but blind to the external world. They stared ahead of her but the sight was focused inwards, perceiving only her internal balance. When she arrived at a motionless body she moved with the natural malevolence of pure energy. There was none of the childlike triumph of life that the other dancers conveyed, only pure movement vanquishing stillness. When her own stillness returned there was no sense of loss, no illogical sorrow, as there had been with the others when they sank back into their deathlike trance. Her return to stillness was shocking for its coldness, nothing more than an abstract contradiction of movement. There was no loss, only transformation from one condition to its antithesis.

Her solo negated the infusion of narrative and drama that the other dancers had almost accidentally brought to the piece. It denied the story of life and death that the audience had colluded with, and presented the entire piece anew as an abstraction of form and structure. It tore away everything but the spatial, stripping the audience of the story it wanted to be told.

The piece that Stuart saw that night had been choreographed with Frances in mind. A visiting American choreographer had seen her perform several times in practice pieces at the school, and built his ballet around her cold, precise, instrumentality. He rehearsed the Company without telling her or any of the other members of her central role. He simply made sure that Frances had the final solo and rehearsed no more than the steps with the dancers. When they asked him about his intention, the meaning behind the piece, he merely requested that each of them aim for precision. He knew that all but Frances would carry their humanity into the ballet without being told, and that, if he had asked them to do otherwise, they would have only half-succeeded. He also knew that, had he asked Frances to dance a narrative, her movements would have been awkward with misuse. He got precisely the effect he wanted by allowing Frances and the rest to be what they couldn't avoid being.

It was as if he had written a concerto for a harpsichord

and full orchestra, allowing the colour and warmth of the orchestrated sound to show up the cool linear geometry of a succession of pure single notes.

Frances's dancing had been noticed and admired, but there was always some hesitation in the enthusiasm; an unspoken dislike of the immaculate control she exhibited. There was a lack at what most people instinctively felt should be the centre. She was likened once to a Stradivarius that played itself: note perfect, but without the thrilling, telling danger, of fallible, individual human fingers.

Frances conveyed what she knew herself to be and the audience accepted it. Form without content, organless, a solid entity of muscle wrapped about a central core of skeleton. It was this mental image of herself that gave her the power and control that the other dancers in the Company could never achieve, hampered as they were with soft parts, emotions and moods that inevitably flawed, or humanized (depending how you looked at it), their performance.

That was how the world saw Frances when she danced. Stuart saw it too, but missed the point. He watched her and was transfixed. His skin began to prick as the old pain and longing welled up in him: redoubled. He saw what everyone else saw, what everyone else admired but couldn't like. But he saw more, or less, than everyone else in the audience. He imagined a heart beating beneath the body ribcage, and the glistening ruby hair loose about her shoulders. He pictured the inward-looking eyes refocused and warm, looking out and taking in, and the smooth, lean face creased with expression.

His fantasies, as he sat there in the darkness, were unaccountable. He conjured her possibilities out of nowhere. Frances on stage was complete and self-contained, a creature of the present moment. There was no hint about her of past or future. Stuart was lost again, deep in an old dream that would have seemed ridiculous and hopelessly inappropriate to anyone else in the auditorium who gazed at the last motionless icon in the spotlight.

As the clapping died away Stuart squeezed past the row of people helping each other on with coats, and beginning their assessment of the performance. He stood patiently in the foyer of the stage entrance waiting for Frances to emerge. He was going to tell her once again that he loved her, and make her see, really see, what he was saying. He knew how much was inside her, how connected they were. He had to explain to her, finally, that they *had* to be together, to be each other's family. They belonged, and she, gradually, would come to see that and become truly herself.

'Frances,' Stuart began, leaning across the table in the nearby Indian restaurant. 'Listen to me . . .'

Her face was scrubbed clean of make-up, the skin glowing and gleaming slightly from a thin layer of moisturizer. Her hair was loose and hung, straight and weighty, on either side of her shoulders. Everyone had turned to look as they settled themselves at the table. She was uncharacteristically fidgety and excited. Stuart put it down to the after-effects of the performance.

She cut across his sentence.

'I'm leaving the flat.' She kept her eyes on his face, wide and steady. 'I'm moving in with Seymour.'

Stuart stared back at her. Still fluttering around his head, like scraps of litter in the wind, were the phrases from which he had to select to persuade her to see sense. 'I love you . . . I want you . . . we must be together properly . . . you're so full . . . there's so much in you . . . if you tried . . . I know it would work out . . . I don't care if you don't love me immediately . . .'

'Did you hear me?' she demanded. 'I'm moving out.'

'Who is Seymour?'

'The piece you saw tonight – he wrote it. He's a choreographer. We've been – involved – for weeks. I'm going to live with him.'

'I was going to ask you to marry me,' Stuart said quietly. A fact, a might-have-been, not an effort to persuade.

'That would have been silly. You know what I'm like. You've had ten years of knowing what I'm like, and after seeing me perform . . .'

'What do you mean?'

'That's why I wanted you to come tonight. I thought if you saw me dance you'd realize, you'd stop hoping I was someone else . . .' She shrugged and then shot a look of anger at him. 'How *could* you still want me after seeing the performance?'

'There's more to you than that. That bloke, that Seymour, doesn't know you. He used part of you and ignored the rest. You can't go and live with someone who thinks that's what you are.'

'He knows me, you don't. You're very hard to explain things to.'

Stuart looked down at the white linen tablecloth and watched his dreams dissipate, wafting away on the air like the scented steam from the pilau rice cooling on the table between them. Frances sat straight and still, waiting to be released from the sadness in Stuart's eyes. After a moment he raised them. They had the false, bright look of someone who had just seen off a loved-one on a train that had now receded too far into the distance; there was nothing more to look at, only a pin-point that was no better than a memory. Time to turn away and walk back down the platform.

When he spoke it was in meaningless monosyllables designed to fill the silence. His anger and disappointment skulked behind the clipped sounds like caged animals.

'Well. OK. So be it.'

'Amen.' She smiled slightly, offering him a weary camaraderie, a shrug, a raised eyebrow of inevitability. But still she waited. They were imprisoned, the two of them, across the table, waiting for the energy to burst and set them free. Frances held on to her breath as if her building need for air would force his explosion. Eventually, it worked; Stuart snapped.

'Fuck you. You fucking bitch. Lying, narcissistic, self-centred cow. You've done nothing but use me. You never cared, not when we were kids, not now. You're right, there isn't anything to you. There's nothing there. I've wasted half my life loving you and there's nothing there to love. I don't care if you go, good riddance. To hell with you.'

He stood as he spoke, pushing the table at Frances to free himself. She inhaled, filling her starving lungs with air and Stuart's angry words, grateful that the moment had come. She stopped herself from saying that she had always told him the truth; that, even so, she was sorry; that, in a way, she loved him and would miss him. She had no right to say any of it, he had every right to say what he was saying. It didn't matter, anyway, the thing was done at last. She didn't really care.

'Do you love me?' she asked.

Frances lay curled with her back to Seymour, nestled in his arms, and feeling the damp flesh of his chest and thighs beginning to cool her own body. Seymour raised his face from the mass of tangled red hair, blowing the strands away from his mouth and nose. He craned his neck to see her profile.

'Not for one second.'

Frances kept her eyes shut and smiled.

'Promise?'

'I swear it on the American Constitution and my mother's life.'

'And you never will?'

'Not a chance. All I want from you, kid, is your body — sexually and choreographically. Not necessarily in that order.'

'You don't think,' she twisted her torso round to scrutinize his face, 'I've got inner qualities? Submerged, you know, but,' she screwed up her eyes, '*there*.'

He took the uppermost nipple into his mouth and sucked on it, making appreciative noises.

'Mmm. Huh uh,' he came up for air. 'It's the outer qualities I like. The day I so much as glimpse an inner quality, you're out on your ear. What I like about you, my cold, empty darling,' he returned to her breast, 'is your wonderful . . . uncomplicated . . . supple . . . strong. . . . dancer's body.' He sat up. 'You fuck like a dancer and you dance like a dancer.

153

Let me tell you, they're both short careers. I'm going to make the most of them while I can.'

'I don't know how you got your reputation as an intellectual. You're so coarse.'

'I lie, babe. And I'm also *very* charismatic. Turn round and I'll show you. Oh, shit,' he said as he caught sight of his watch. 'We've got to go to work. Rehearsals begin at ten. I'll show you later.' He jumped out of bed and made for the bathroom. 'God, what city are we in?' he called from the hall. 'No, don't tell me. It's Paris, right? Yeah, it's Paris, I can smell the leftover scent of tear gas and blocked drains. Maybe we should go and chuck a few cobblestones at the gendarmerie. We could do it on the way to the theatre, it would save time on warm-up exercises. Are you up yet?' Frances heard the sound of water flushing and a tap running.

She swung herself out of bed and called, 'London, we're in London. You got back yesterday. You haven't told me how Mireille was.'

Seymour came back into the room, rubbing his dark beard dry with a towel. He leaned against the wall and watched as Frances climbed into her practice clothes.

'I've got to cut down on the dope, it's very bad for a person's sense of geography. Mireille was fine.' He watched her carefully over the towel. 'That's not jealousy I detect in your voice, is it? We had a deal, remember? I don't do the fidelity bit.'

Frances grabbed her hair at the nape of her neck and twisted it around her hand before clipping it firmly at the back of her head.

'That's OK, I wouldn't want you to. I just wondered how Mireille was.'

Seymour narrowed his eyes.

'She was fine. And she's a great fuck. Listen, I sleep with other chicks, right? That's how it is.'

Frances smiled gently at him.

'You sound as if you want me to be jealous. I'm not. I'm delighted that Mireille's a great fuck.' She paused for a second and bent down to straighten the back seam of her footless tights. 'But she can't dance as well as me.'

Seymour threw the towel on to the bed and broke into a huge grin; his white, carefully tended American teeth shone between the surrounding blackness of his beard. He crossed the room and took Frances in his arms.

'Nobody dances as well as you, baby.' He laughed, releasing the twist of hair from its clip and running his fingers through it, loosening and freeing the strands. 'And, right now, there's no one I want to fuck more than you. Let's go back to bed.'

It was 1968, almost two years since Frances had left Stuart's flat. Seymour had built his own company around Frances and they toured Europe with the ballets he devised, all of them formalist abstractions. At cultural symposia at the Round House, the Arts Lab and the ICA, Seymour described what he was attempting.

'We are exploring the Archimedes Principle in the realm of movement. The solid structure of the body displacing empty space. The opposing conditions of the full and the empty. Solid matter confronting the immaterial, and form opposing form. The real story is without story; it is patterns of balance and imbalance between object and the void, between gravity and the power of locomotion, between the energy of muscle and entropy.'

Although his talks were greatly improved by being in French, the audiences everywhere they went, though small, were rapt. And if the words themselves meant little when subjected to serious scrutiny, Frances in performance gave them substance when with her icy precision she moved across the vacant spaces of the stage.

Frances was neither happy nor content. She was, though, as near as she had ever been to what she wanted to be – oblivious, in a tiny world of her own making. She worked at her performance and lived, when she was not dancing, in a kind of dream. Seymour, there and not there, rushed about and organized and did the talking. He was like a sprite, small and strong, shorter than Frances by several inches, and covered with dark hair. His clever, almost cunning face was submerged behind his beard and thick mane, but the brilliant, dark eyes shone out, always gleaming with energy. He arranged Frances's steps on stage, and seemed also to arrange her stillness off it. Dancing, practice, daily life with Seymour were a continuum. It was all the same piece of work: abstract and choreographed. He moved around, met people, arranged things, slept with pretty passing girls, or old lovers in other cities, but without imposing difficulty on Frances. She worked, she was tired, Seymour was there or not there. There was nothing to care about except getting the performance right.

Off stage, Frances drifted quietly through her life. She wore long floating skirts, patch-dyed, loose blouses with long, wide sleeves shaped like arum lilies, and scarves, twisted and flowing around her neck, tied bandanna-style around her forehead. She spoke very little and smiled people enigmatically away when they came too near. Seymour's friends were uneasy about her. They sat on cushions in smoke-filled rooms whose air made you stoned just by being in them, discussing art and philosophy, arguing the relative merits of minimalism and pop art, arms waving, tempers rising, but always aware, in the corner of their eyes, of the languid girl who watched them in silence. She took and smoked the joints they passed to her, but her smile only became more indecipherable while their voices rose and their arguments became too intricate for even themselves to follow. She would lie against Seymour and let him play with her long, finely plaited hair while he expounded on some nice point of abstract expressionism. Or she would sit alone, curled on a large cushion, unmoved when Seymour had some other body leaning against his to toy with. But no one was quite able to dismiss her as one of the passive, vacant girls that lay around silently in a cannabis stupor while their men propounded theories. There was something too alert, too judgemental beneath the stillness.

For her part, Frances simply watched, and listened only intermittently – there wasn't much to hear. She was allowing time to pass. Waiting, not for something to happen, but for the passage of time. She smoked dope, but carefully, mindful of what the ether dreams had become. She found the com-

156

pany discomforting. There never seemed to be a roomful of people with whom she felt at ease. They were always visitors, or she was, and she waited for them to leave from the moment they arrived.

In bed with Seymour she would weave her limbs around him; an elegant, active lover.

'Jesus, you were quiet tonight,' he'd whisper. 'Why don't you ever talk to anyone?'

'I thought I'd save my conversation for you,' she'd respond, running her fingers up his inner thigh. 'What would you like to talk about? The dialectics of schizophrenia, censorship and the media, Brook's interpretation of The Empty Space?'

'Let's talk about why you turn from the Mona Fucking Lisa in the living-room into Mae Fucking West in the bedroom,' Seymour would whisper between sharp intakes of breath as she ran a delicate fingernail around the contours of his testicles.

'Power. The politics of desire. Now there's a topic of conversation,' she'd say, snaking slowly down the bed.

'Forget the talk, just keep heading in the direction you're going.'

Late one night early in the New Year Frances stood staring at her reflection in the window. Frances watching Frances in the dark glass. Seymour was away for a few days. Outside, the snow was falling. Her reflection had the quality of an old, silent film, scored with scratches on the celluloid. She stood quite still and re-focused for a moment on the night and the falling snow beyond the glass. The flakes drifted roughly downward, deflecting sometimes to the left or right before continuing their fall, taking casual detours as if gravity, though finally the victor, must wait. The effort of trying to see a single pattern in the wayward dance of the snow made her dizzy. Her brain recognized the phrase, 'it is snowing', but her eyes insisted on seeing separate flakes on intricate journeys.

She was disturbed from her trance by the ring of the doorbell.

All she could make of her visitor, standing in the doorway, was how much there was of her. Jumpers, coats, hat, scarves, boots, tights, gloves – several of each, it seemed. Everything was piled on top of each other, their frantic colours and patterns – Afghan, Indian, Icelandic, Moroccan, Fair Isle – dancing like spots in front of her eyes. The only part that was exposed to the world were the eyes, rimmed red and tear-laden from the driving snow, peering out between the layers of damp wool, the surrounding flesh of the lids and upper cheeks raging scarlet from the cold. The eyes looked shocked, terrorized, as human eyes do when faced with Nature's total lack of concern for those who like to think of themselves as her children. The rest of her – it was obviously a female apparition – looked ridiculous, standing there like a door-to-door jumble sale as if she were waiting for Frances to pounce on some particularly choice item.

Frances stared without saying anything. She couldn't believe that this multicoloured bundle could be one of Seymour's girlfriends.

'Frances, it's me.' The voice was muffled by several thicknesses of sodden wool, but faintly familiar. The figure unpeeled a layer of scarf and sniffed her runny rose under control. She began to unwind the twisted scarves and pull away the hat and balaclava that covered her head.

'It's Sandra,' she said, when her neck and face were finally revealed. 'You remember, from school?'

Frances wouldn't have recognised her without the prompt. Her hair, that had been thick and long, was cropped close to her head, clumsily shorn like the victim of a persecution. It had once been richly golden; now it was just pallid and dirty-looking, matching her face. Frances stared as the rest of the outer clothing came off. The real change was in her weight. What had been a sensuous, roundly curving body was fleshless, like a starved, winter bird. Her face was gaunt, all dark hollows, the skin patterned with rough, red patches.

'I'm sorry, I know it's late. I got your address from your father. He didn't know your phone number. I'll go if it's not convenient . . . only I haven't got . . .'

Frances realized they were still standing in the doorway. She took an armful of clothes from Sandra's hands and then wondered what to do with the saturated bundle.

'Come in. I'm sorry. It's such a surprise . . . I didn't . . .'

'I know, I've changed.'

'Sit down. How are you?' Frances took the clothes into the bathroom and dumped them in the bath. She returned and joined Sandra on the bank of cushions that lined one wall of the room.

'You look wonderful,' Sandra smiled. 'So much more yourself. I've heard about you. You're a successful dancer. I knew you'd be all right.'

Frances watched her shivering in the warm flat.

'Look, why don't you have a bath and warm up? You can wear something of mine. You're soaked.'

'I walked here from the station, from Euston.'

Euston was three or four miles away.

'Could I have a bath? I'd really like one. It's ages since I last had a bath.'

Half an hour later Sandra came into the living-room wrapped in a towel. The bones at her neck and shoulders jutted frighteningly, the skin that covered them was stretched and paper-thin, whitened from the pressure of sharp bone. Frances handed her some jeans and a jumper.

'Here, put these on. I've made an omelette and some coffee.'

She watched Sandra tear into the omelette and get through five slices of bread and butter before pausing to gulp down half the coffee. Frances filled her cup and cut more bread.

'When did you last eat?'

Sandra laughed nervously, losing some of her mouthful. She swallowed and giggled again.

'Honestly, I can't remember. In Norwich, I think. I had a sandwich.' She glanced at Frances and popped the fallen bread back into her mouth. 'I stole it from the café on the station. Someone had left it there while they went to get something else from the counter. Actually, it was only half a sandwich.'

'What's happened to you?' Frances asked, hardly wanting to hear the answer as she poured more coffee into Sandra's empty cup.

'You're so kind. You always were. Remember how you

used to do my essays for me? I'm sorry to dump myself on you like this. I didn't have anywhere else to go.'

'Your parents?'

'No,' Sandra shook her head briskly. 'I don't see them any more. Well, I couldn't even if they wanted to see me. Not the way I am. My brother gave me some money once or twice, but then he wouldn't any more. He said . . . It doesn't matter, it's my fault, the way I am.'

'But what happened to you? You were going to secretarial college . . .'

Sandra sniffed. The warmth and her full belly had loosened her mucous membrane; her nose was beginning to stream. Frances fetched her some loo paper from the bathroom.

'I didn't do very well there. Well, it was all right, I passed the exams, more or less, but not well.' She smiled up at Frances as she dabbed at her nose. 'I didn't have you there to help me out. Anyway, I got a job, but nothing fancy. Just a sort of filing clerk. My parents weren't impressed. You can imagine. And I couldn't stand living with my aunt. She was a real cow. Then I got pregnant again by this bloke in the office. My boss. Married, of course. But he was nice to me. Before, I mean.'

'Didn't you use any contraception?'

'I didn't seem to get round to sorting anything out. I suppose I thought he'd marry me. God knows why. Well, he didn't, but he did pay for an abortion and then he sacked me. When my aunt found out, she threw me out. She said I was a tart. That kind of thing. I couldn't face going back to my parents. I got on a train and met this bloke. He was going to Norwich, he had a flat there . . .'

She fell silent for a moment. Frances wished it were the end of the story.

'Let's go next door. It's more comfortable.'

They sat side by side on the cushions watching the snow falling outside the window. Sandra was still shivering, Frances saw; she couldn't still be cold.

'Who was he, this man?'

'Just a bloke.' She lapsed into silence again for a moment and began to pick at the edges of her fingernails. 'He was a junkie.' She continued to stare down at her almost frantic hands. 'He hustled, sold H, you know.' She looked up at Frances for a moment. 'Just for the bread, to get enough to live and for his stuff. He wasn't a professional,' she assured Frances, who wanted very much not to hear the rest of the story.

'How long were you with him?' she asked.

'A year and a half, two years. Something like that. Until yesterday. He handed me this ticket to London and told me to leave. Thing is, I started using too. I don't know, it seemed all right. Everybody was. And Dave was so together, you know? He didn't seem like a junkie at all. He was always careful about eating properly and wearing decent clothes. And there was something amazing about the way he fixed. It was sort of hypnotizing, magical. If he was in a room full of people, and started to get his gear out, everyone would go silent and watch him until he'd finished, like it was a performance or something. You'd watch him drawing the blood into the works and then push the plunger very slowly in and out, and you couldn't stop looking until it was over.' Sandra seemed lost in the memory, captivated by an inner visualization of the moment she described.

'What did you do for money?'

Sandra came to and shrugged.

'Anything. He sold stuff, but it wasn't enough for the two of us. I stole things. Cheque books were the best, but anything that could be sold was all right. And sometimes, well, you know, you'll do anything. I'd pick up blokes who paid me. But recently . . . I've got so thin . . . you know . . . no one was really interested. And then Dave got this new chick.' Sandra sighed and blew her nose on the wad of loo paper she held crushed in one hand.

'Look, I'm sorry to lay this on you. But I didn't know what else to do. Thing is, I'm really stuck.' She began shivering again, but more violently now. 'I haven't had a fix since I left Norwich. I used the last at the station and I haven't got any money.' Tears began to roll slowly down her cheeks. 'I don't know what to do.'

She began trembling as a wracking need took over from the cold and hunger she had felt.

'What can I do?' Frances asked. 'I've got some money, but I don't know where we'd get heroin at this time of night. I mean, I don't know anyone . . . What about a doctor?'

Sandra shook her head fiercely.

'I've got some dope. Would a joint help?'

'No,' Sandra shivered. 'It just gives me a headache. If you could let me have some money I could get some stuff. I'm sorry. I'll try and pay you back. Really.'

'Do you know anyone in London to sell it to you?'

'I know of some places I've heard about. But it'd be difficult getting there now. Have you got any sleepers? If I could stay the night, in the morning I'd be able to find something. Sleepers would help tonight.'

'I've got barbiturates. Would a couple of Seconal get you through?'

Sandra laughed shakily.

'Maybe if I shot them up. Give me four.'

'Couldn't you try and see a doctor? You look so ill.' Frances handed her the pills with a glass of water and made up the cushions into a comfortable bed.

'No, they'd put me away. Listen,' she said as she undressed and got under the blankets, 'I'm really grateful for this. It's great to see you again. You look so good and the flat's . . . really nice. I'm sorry I'm in such a state. I'd like to talk to you properly. About you, how you're getting on and everything. In the morning, let's talk.' She was beginning to sound sleepy. 'You can tell me everything you're doing and what's been happening to you. You've done so well. I am pleased for you.'

Frances checked that she was asleep and then turned off the lights before going to bed herself.

She lay in the dark and decided that she would call a doctor anyway, in the morning. Sandra looked to her as if there was barely a thread of life left in her. She couldn't let her leave in that condition wandering around London looking for heroin. She remembered Sandra at school. It just wasn't the same person. Physically, there was nothing left of the unconscious beauty that had made the air shimmer as she passed through it. But there had been something, even then – the pain, Frances supposed, her terrible need to do what she couldn't do, a kind of hunger in her voice – that connected with the pathetic wraith that slept in her living-room trying not to feel the withdrawal that wracked her ruined body. Even so, it was almost impossible to put the memory of Sandra together with the bag of skin and bone next door. She got up and crept into the bathroom to find a Seconal to get herself to sleep.

Frances walked into the living-room determined to make Sandra see a doctor. The blankets were thrown back over the empty cushions. She called out and looked in the kitchen. It was empty. Her purse lay open on the kitchen table, a few pennies scattered around it. Fifteen pounds were gone and some change. She wandered about the flat noticing what was missing. A fountain pen, and her cheque book, from her bag; a couple of gold and opal rings she kept on her dressing-table; some clothes, jumpers, blouses, a trouser suit and a coat. Frances, not used to sleeping pills, had stayed asleep while Sandra went through her wardrobe. A couple of newish record albums had gone, West Coast stuff: the Jefferson Airplane, Captain Beefheart, she thought. Except for the cheque book and the rings there was nothing really valuable in the flat. Most of the stuff she'd taken would have sold for a few shillings.

Frances made herself some coffee and called her bank. She told them she had lost her cheque book the night before, somewhere in Leicester Square. They said they would put a stop on the cheques. Then she folded the blankets and put them back in the bathroom cupboard. The rest of the bottle of Seconal had gone too, she noticed.

She sat on the edge of the bath and tried to remember something that Stuart had said to her once, when they were still at school. 'You'll survive,' he'd said, or something like that, 'while the rest of us fall apart.' It was true. She had thought once that by not caring she was making disaster

163

come to her, speeding towards catastrophe and then oblivion. But it hadn't worked like that. She had survived although she thought she was trying not to. By not caring she'd survived. She had put herself in the way of disaster or emptiness but always it had skittered past her, slid around her, avoided contact. It *was* funny, as Stuart had said, a bad joke that it was Sandra out there, desperate and dying on the street and she, Frances, who sat in her flat cancelling her cheque book and counting the losses. It didn't matter how absent from the world she tried to become, she was still a big success, a credit to her mother.

My daughter, the dancer. Nice flat, nice life, travels, not short of money, and so many interesting friends.

Congratulations, Mrs Pepper. Well done, Mr Pepper, for bringing up such a successful member of the human race. All your sacrifices were worth it. Hasn't she done well? Isn't she a lovely girl? You must be very proud, the two of you, of what you've made. She's a lucky girl, but not just lucky, success in life has to be worked for too. It doesn't just happen by accident. You can't tell me she didn't work for it, strive for the satisfactory life she has. She had ambition, your girl, a real will to succeed.

A will to survive. Frances knew finally that had to be true. She was nauseous at the thought. Her stomach heaved violently. She just had time to lean over to the basin before she began to vomit.

– Go on, why have you stopped?

– Is it necessary to go on to the absolute end?

– You finally got around to starting, you'll have to get around to finishing.

– I feel a great weariness.

– The end's in sight. That's always difficult.

– How the hell do you know?

– I feel I've grown close to you. We're in this together, after all.

– The hell we are. The only character that exists round here is me. Me in my very own private cosmos. No one gets in and I don't get out. You, you're just a dream I thought I'd have.

– You mention hell a lot. Does it frighten you?

– No. I don't believe in it. I've got nothing to believe with, remember? I don't believe in you either.

– Never mind, I'll believe in me for both of us. It's remarkable how real a dream can be when it's needed badly enough.

– I don't need anything. I just wish it was all over.

– You or the story?

– Do you want to hear another of my mother's short stories?

– Yes. Perhaps the break will do you good.

– Look, could you drop the avuncular tone? I may be young but I'm approaching the end of my days. Don't patronize me. I'll tell you the story. Maybe the break will do me good. It's called:

ISN'T IT ROMANTIC?

Yesterday a man walked into a newsagent's shop and bought a morning paper. It doesn't matter which. As the man was

165

leaving he heard, although he was hardly aware of it, the newsagent humming to himself as he shuffled the piles of papers back into order.

The tune he was humming was 'Isn't It Romantic?' It goes: dum de dum de *dum dum*, dum de dum de *dum dum dum*. And so on. It's a famous song, of the Thirties I think, although perhaps it was a decade earlier or later. I'm not sure. I also think it was in a film starring Fred Astaire. I don't know which one, but I suppose that would make it the Thirties. Anyway, it's not important.

The man left the shop and walked towards the bus stop that he waited at every morning to get to work. Whatever he did for a living, it didn't pay enough for him to have a car. Or perhaps he worked in town and was worried about getting caught by one of the new traffic wardens. He sat on the top deck of the bus when it came and the bus conductor heard him whistling 'Isn't It Romantic?' to himself as he climbed the stairs to get the new fares. God knows what everyone had to whistle or hum about.

The bus conductor got the tune on his mind and la-la-la'ed it as he walked about giving out tickets.

A woman passenger picked it up, although she thought she'd thought of it herself and hummed it as she looked in a butcher's shop window, wondering what to buy for supper. (You notice, we've got back to humming again. There are only so many ways of expressing music apart from full-throated singing.)

A passing drunk caught the tune and it rolled around in his dizzy head reminding him of something he'd forgotten all about. He sang it at the top of his voice, until he remembered what it reminded him of, and then he began to cry.

That must have been when I heard it through the open window of the room I was in, thinking about whether or not to write a story. But I didn't register it because I have no recollection of thinking about the song at all for the rest of the day or night. This morning, though, I woke with the tune of 'Isn't It Romantic?' all ready and waiting to be sung. Which is what I did while I made myself a cup of tea. 'Isn't it rom *an tic*, dum de dum de *dum dum dum*.' I could only remember the words of the first line, so I la-la-la'ed the rest like the bus conductor.

That's all really. Except to say that of all those people

166

who'd gone about singing 'Isn't It Romantic?', I was the only one who knew the whole story of how I came to be singing it. That's because I wrote the story.

– Well, at least it was short. She might have traced the damn thing back for a week.

– Or a month, or to the Thirties.

– Did Frances only laugh in her stories?

– I suppose that was why she wrote them. She would have laughed at other things but she forgot a lot of the time. And when she did laugh she discovered that she was the only one. Other people seemed to find different things funny. Bit out of step, my mother. It must be said that not many people found her stories funny, although she laughed all the time she was writing them.

– Did you find them funny?

– Oh yes, I laughed myself silly behind my wild, blue eyes. I wish I could have told her.

– You had much in common, you two.

– Everything except pain and rage. They were all hers.

– And your father? Did you have much in common with him? You did have a father, I suppose?

– Naturally. You're a figment of *my* imagination, not the other way round. Of course, I had a father. It's just that he wanted me dead. I can understand that. Everyone did, except Mother. It makes her a little special to me. But I'm coming to that.

– You're ready to go on then?

– To the bitter end.

FRANCES TURNED ON both taps and watched the water flush the basin clear. She felt the weight of something black and putrefying replace the space in her emptied stomach, rising and filling her to capacity with its mass. It was familiar now, almost a friend. It was time for another refusal. Time to turn her back and walk away. It was still necessary to demonstrate – to herself? to Them? to Her? – that she knew, as ever, the absurdity of it all, the pointlessness. To show, and to know that, still, she didn't care. She thought about the missing bottle of Seconal and considered the gas taps on the oven, but with distaste. Too positive. Open to the cosy interpretation that she cared too much, easy for the living to reject the possibility that she cared not at all. Drama and self-inflicted death evoked tragedy. That wasn't it.

She turned off the taps, went back into the living-room and picked up the phone.

'Stuart? You're still there, then? Can we meet? What about lunch at the Indian place, you know, where we . . . right, that's the one.' It was nearly two years since she had last seen him.

'Do you still want to marry me?' she demanded, leaning forward over her folded arms. There was only challenge present in her raised eyebrows and faintly curved mouth.

Stuart didn't hesitate.

'I love you, you know that.'

'But do you still want to marry me?' she asked again, sweeping his love aside.

She gazed at him, perplexed, while he replied in a voice rock-solid with certainty.

'I want to be with you. I always will. I don't care about

168

getting married, the ceremony thing, the piece of paper. But I want to *be married* to you.'

Frances shrugged and opened her clasped hands, spreading her fingers like petals on a flower.

'All right then. You can't say you don't know what you are getting into.'

Stuart just stared at her.

'I said I'll marry you,' she repeated.

'Are you sure?' Stuart suddenly felt he needed armour, that a blow was coming.

'Yes. Completely.'

'But you said you didn't love me, that you'd never love me.'

'I don't love you. I said I'd marry you. Take it or leave it.'

Stuart waited for an explanation.

'I don't want children. I can't marry you unless you accept that. And I'm giving up dancing. You'll have to support me, I'm afraid, but I won't cost much. And I don't suppose I'll be very different, any nicer than I've always been, but I won't try deliberately to hurt you. But if I'm going to be dependent on you, you'll have to give up the revolution and the sabotage and stuff and settle for being an ordinary, electrical engineer with a wife to support.'

'Mechanical,' he said mechanically.

'Whatever. Do you agree? Those are the terms. It's up to you.'

Stuart couldn't take it all in: all the pieces were too big to absorb.

'How can you give up dancing? Why? You're just at the beginning of a brilliant career. I've seen you. I've been to all of your performances in London. You should be a dancer.'

She shook her hair back over her shoulders.

'Yes, well, I've had enough. I'm going to become a wife. Can we buy a house in the suburbs?'

'But if you don't love me . . . and what about Seymour?'

'Seymour was about dancing, and I'm not dancing any more. I'm fond of you. I wouldn't dream of marrying someone I loved; if that's something you have to have, we won't do it.'

'What will you do all day in this house in the suburbs?'

He had the same feeling of unreality he got when someone told the story of a movie he hadn't seen. It always sounded too improbable to exist.

'Cook, clean the house, garden, read magazines, prepare dinner parties for your colleagues. I'll go for walks in the afternoon. I'm going to be a housewife.'

'But no children?'

'No.'

'And my political commitments?'

'Are out. Well, I suppose you can join the Labour Party if you have to. You could become a local councillor or something, but nothing fancy, nothing that'll threaten our domestic bliss. We each have to give up something. I'm giving up dancing, you give up the revolution. I think that's a balanced sacrifice, don't you?'

Stuart faced the possibility that he was going to get what he had always wanted – in a way. But something told him that that was always how one got what one wanted.

He was surprised to find that the idea of severing his connection with the comrades was not impossible to imagine. He had been certain that his commitment was absolute. In the last eighteen months he had fought with police, broken down the fencing in Grosvenor Square, called noisily for the victory by the NLF and been arrested several times. The army of liberation had grown strong against American imperialism. The stage was set, everyone was convinced, for the collapse of the forces of state repression. The time had come. Everything suggested that they, the people everywhere – in Britain, France, the US, Vietnam – were finally going to break through and win.

Now he sat open-mouthed, contemplating a bourgeois existence in the suburbs, a house, a wife, a steady job, and he discovered to his astonishment that he could walk away from the forthcoming revolution, and that he was no longer certain that it was the answer. He was no longer certain what the question had been in the first place.

What had seemed a solid core dispersed into a haze as the old core re-emerged: Frances, whatever she was.

He counted the years. Twelve years old on the bombsite; fifteen, watching her around the school; seventeen, eighteen, supplying her with oblivion, aiding and abetting her attempts to get locked up; twenty, twenty-one, twenty-two, supporting her flight into the other kind of oblivion of dancing. Frances – always nearby and unattainable. He didn't fool himself for a moment that now he had achieved what he wanted, that Frances, after his years of patience and devotion, had suddenly become his and learned to love him as he loved her. There were, as ever, two levels in her dealings with him. He might accompany her along her chosen route but he never caught the whispered, private monologue that was her real existence. She might marry him, but her motives, her intentions, were her own, and had very little to do with Stuart himself. He knew that. It was a pain he had accepted long ago.

But he also had a core of hope. He still believed that time would heal the rift between her actions and intentions. The edifices would wear away with time and his care to reveal what he had always known was there. He would wait for as long as it took. One day, she would notice him and when she did he would be there, on the spot, wedded and waiting, to reap the benefit. He was a believer, he knew that eventually it would all come right.

Frances performed as she had promised. She bought recipe books and learned to cook proper meals. She filled the cupboard in the kitchen with dusters, polishes and sprays. She took walks in the local park in the afternoon while the dinner simmered. She was an efficient and pleasant hostess, and if she were a trifle distant it was no more than enough to give her an interesting edge in the culs-de-sac of Chislehurst. She gave the neighbours and Stuart's new colleagues the impression that she was myopic, although she didn't wear glasses. But she seemed to peer at them, as if she were continually trying to bring them into focus. They felt confused by her stare. If no one looked at them so closely, no one made them feel so invisible. When Frances gazed at them intently over the dinner table, or across her sherry glass, they felt, obscurely, that they were no longer there.

Stuart knew the feeling. He was used to it. But he waited, and wasn't discontent with his new life. Occasionally he made suggestions.

'Perhaps you should get a job – an outside interest. What about teaching dance?'

'No, everything's fine as it is.'

'You should read more. Why not study something?'

She shook her head and smiled.

They lived their suburban dream for five years. Stuart got promotion. He was reliable and talented. He was going to go far. He did join the local Labour Party and was soon elected on to the local council where he got a reputation for being an honest, trustworthy campaigner for worthwhile local issues. He battled conscientiously to preserve the green belt, against pollution, for the provision of new council housing, and made a difference. People went to him and listened to him. He had respect. It was thought when he had served his apprenticeship that he would have the makings of a fine MP.

But he had not broken through the amiable carapace of his wife. Their life together was pleasant and, in bed, she still made sex seem like an exploration. She encouraged his fantasies, suggested things that he had half a mind for anyway. She allowed his curiosity to play and expand.

One morning she lay in bed watching him shave in the adjoining bathroom.

'Why don't you grow a beard?' she asked idly.

'I think shaving turns me on,' he slurred through his contorted mouth. 'I like watching the clear skin coming through the foam.'

'Come and shave me, then.'

It was a thought that had occurred to him more than once. She lay still, adjusting her legs as he happily spread on shaving foam and scraped her pubic mound smooth and naked.

He worked away with the professional concentration of a barber.

'There's a bit here . . . it's very hard to get at. Whatever you do, don't move.'

'I knew I'd be grateful for all that dance training. Do you fancy doing my armpits when you've finished that?'

'Armpits are for another day. I'm planning to enjoy the fruits of my labour. Would Madam like a little aftershave?'

Another time she turned over and offered her buttocks to the belt he was thoughtfully pulling out of the trousers he had just taken off.

'Go on then,' she smiled over her shoulder.

'I'm not into that sort of thing,' he said even more thoughtfully. 'It doesn't do a thing for me.'

'Then why are you still holding your belt?'

'So it doesn't do anything for you, huh?' she asked after he had laid a couple of tentative blows on her, and they both gazed with curiosity at his growing erection.

'Christ,' he murmured, 'do you think I should see a shrink?'

'No. Let's see what happens if I do it to you.'

'Christ,' he said again, a few moments later. 'I'll make an appointment tomorrow.'

'I think,' Frances laughed, climbing on top of him, 'that you're a really balanced human being.'

It was the old game being played, from way back on the bombsite. It was only that this time the walls were higher, and he was allowed to start in the same room. It was enjoyable, exciting. But all the 'What if's . . .' and 'Why don't you's . . .' and 'Let's try's . . .' amounted to a game that could only be played if he submerged his real passion, his unwanted love for her. She kept his deeper desires at bay with a circus of activity. He didn't complain; he enjoyed the adventures, the open-ended permission. But all along he knew what was missing.

Frances was content. Her life was narrowed to a series of days, none different from the rest. She had boxed herself in and sat quietly in the uneventful darkness, smiling at the void. Let nothing ever happen, she whispered to the vanished child in the vanished space inside her. She was filled with blankness. She was satisfied enough. Some time, she knew with equal satisfaction, she would walk away to find an emptier place to stand. Leaving completed the circle that went nowhere. Nothing should be allowed enough time to develop into something desired.

But after five years something did happen.

'I'm pregnant,' Frances stated one evening as Stuart arrived home.

Not a day of their marriage had passed when Stuart had not had to suppress the urge to suggest a baby to his wife. He wanted children, but, more than that, he had grown increasingly sure that only a child would bring Frances fully into the world. It was a reality that he was sure would make her real. But he dared not suggest it, couldn't risk a confrontation that he knew would send her away. He sent up a soundless prayer of thanks to the fertile goddess of accident.

'I'm very pleased,' he said carefully.

'I'm not. I want an abortion.'

'No.' Suddenly he knew that Frances's willessness would work in his favour. She wouldn't act against the vagaries of chance if he stood absolutely firm. He presented her with a wall of opposition that she would never have the determination to climb. He was right.

Being pregnant shocked all capacity for action out of her. She was astonished to have conceived with a body she knew to be without substance. She had never really believed that she possessed a uterus, or ova, waiting to be filled and fertilized, any more than she could credit herself with heart, lungs or kidneys. She wouldn't have argued with anyone that they were there; she lived and performed all the biological functions that complete human beings were supposed to, but she didn't believe in them, not for her. Pregnancy was impossible: it was too organic a thing to have happened to her. The disbelief rendered her impassive. How could she have become

174

pregnant? How could she have an abortion without acknowledging the treachery of her body, building life where she utterly denied it?

In the meantime, the foetus grew.

The early stages of pregnancy were dark days for Frances.

At first, still numbed with shock, she was intrigued to find her body changing in so precisely the way that bodies are supposed to in pregnancy. Her breasts tingled and she urinated excessively in the first weeks. It interested her that things went so according to the biological blueprint. But gradually, once the novelty of normality had worn off, she began to think of the future as a matter of reality.

She waged a battle against the sentimental fantasies her hormones pumped into her bloodstream. It was a fairly easy victory, given who she was. She hardly allowed herself the smallest daydream of walking hand in hand with her bright, questioning toddler – 'Why is the sky?', 'Where does God pee?' – and heard her amused, honest answers, when the truth elbowed its way to the front of her mind.

She saw, when she was three months pregnant, a vivid, flashing tableau of herself face to face with a solid, adolescent-plump, sour-faced fifteen year old. They stood, each with arms akimbo, foreheads almost touching, in a caricature of confrontation. 'I won't be in by eleven.' 'It's none of your business who I see.' 'I will not do my homework.' And Frances yelling the positive of each of those negatives. 'You will.' 'It is.' 'You will.' Then, 'Why? Why? Why?' And, 'Because – I say so,' repeated to a dying echo.

Frances felt exhausted and terrified at what she couldn't avoid seeing. The image returned again and again to haunt her and drive away the last faint image of a soft, pliant baby, all loving smiles and sleep. And she knew, as she watched the arguing pair repeat their lines over and over, how impossible it would be for her. She wouldn't really care when the great girl came home, or what she did when she was out, and would not, in truth, have any counter to the 'Why should I?' she heard flung at her. There would be no conviction, only the knowledge that she had to say what she had to say, as did the child-woman who faced her.

175

The thought already tired her out. I don't care now, and I won't care then, she thought, imagining the years and years of wearisome play-acting ahead of her.

Frances wasn't equipped for such a long-term enterprise, nor was she able to take things day by day. She needed to know that whatever began would come to an end. She required a completion date for anything she started. For those first twenty-two weeks of pregnancy, she was terrified by the open-endedness of the project.

It was natural to some extent. Anyone might quake at the prospect of parenthood, the seemingly endless obligation of children. Stuart, for example, would have, but he did not allow himself to think in such large chunks of future as Frances. He had that essential quality that allowed the human race to continue in spite of everything, surviving by its blessed capacity for not thinking beyond the immediate prospect. The future, as far as Stuart was concerned, became benign and fuzzy. He never confronted an image of a demanding, necessarily wilful adolescent, or any of the other unattractive or plain dull possibilities that potential parenthood holds. The baby was The Baby. His thoughts were full of Frances with the infant in her arms, milky and maternal, newly weighted to the world and brought down to earth, to the benefit of everyone. He knew, now, that everything would be all right.

But by the twenty-second week of the pregnancy it was clear, even to Stuart, that everything was not going to be all right. Even then, for a brief moment he felt that all was not lost. He altered his mental picture, but managed to come up with another that allowed him to cling to the last thread of hope.

Just as Stuart knew that babies should be normal, he knew that the correct response to one that was not was mutual grief and comfort, prior to aborting the foetus. He expected Frances to cry in his arms, for them both to weep and share the pain of such arbitrary misfortune. He wanted to gain strength from her need for support during the awful necessity of termination and its emotional after-effects. Such was his scenario when they got the news, although it wasn't at all like Frances to behave like that.

She remained adamant. Nothing anyone said moved her. Perhaps adamant is too positive a way of putting it. She was unyielding, but her insistence was completely passive. She stayed quiet in the centre of the emotional storm that raged. Stuart reasoned, bellowed and threatened.

'You can't do this.'

'I can. I am.'

'What for? For Christ's sake, why give birth to a thing without a brain? It's as good as dead already.'

'Aren't we all?'

'This isn't a fucking philosophy seminar. This is *real*, Frances, this is *real*.'

Frances almost smiled.

'Never mind, Stuart, it won't last long.'

'But why? Just tell me why.'

'I feel like it,' Frances said quietly.

Stuart often missed Frances's more elliptical turns of phrase. He didn't catch the truth of this last statement, although it was as near as Frances ever got to an explanation. She identified with what the foetus was more than people with complete brains are supposed to identify with those without them. The coming baby rang true.

Stuart began to shout.

'What about us? Have you thought about us?'

'Us?' Frances said, as if it were the name of someone she had never met.

'I would be the father of this thing. I won't live with it. I won't have anything to do with it.'

'No, I suppose you won't. Shall we have some tea?'

Stuart finally understood that she really intended to go ahead with the pregnancy and, at the same time, that he had lost her. He watched her filling the kettle, the woman he knew changing into the woman he didn't know, had never wanted to know, and realized, very late, that he had never been able to do anything about her. There was that stubborn self-containment that he had been convinced would fall away with time and domesticity and, when that hadn't happened, motherhood, like the moulting of a chrysalis. Inside the imago waited, he had been sure, and that was what he wanted. It was nonsense, of course. He wouldn't have known what to do with Frances falling into his arms, soft and lighter than air. It wasn't what she was for.

Stuart's reaction to Frances's decision to have the baby was hardly more vocal than other people's. Everyone felt that she was going too far.

In fact, the reverse was true. This was as far as Frances could go. The fatally defective baby was just about what she could manage. The truth was that the news came as a great relief. Frances's real terror fell away when the results of the test came through. What she thought, but had had the good sense not so say aloud in the doctor's consulting room, was, thank God.

It was more of a welcome than any brainless infant had a right to expect.

– So we've come to you at last?

– Almost back to the beginning, nearly at the end. It would make me dizzy if I weren't horizontal.

– Poor Stuart.

– Yes. He always was. I never met him, you know. Father. We've never actually breathed the same air.

– He never saw Frances again?

– He visited her sometimes but once I was born he kept in touch by phone. He didn't stop loving her, but he did let go of hope. He dreaded seeing us both together. He didn't want to witness Mother holding me against her. It would have been a parody, you see, of his dreams. The surface image of mother and child. He knew, by then, that it was the brutal reality of death and freedom lying beneath the icon that was precisely what enabled her to behave as tenderly as she did. He couldn't have avoided seeing how the look in her eyes commented sardonically on the gentle smile on her lips, and he wouldn't have been able to stand it. I can't blame him for not wanting to see me. I was what allowed Mother to remain what she was. I had betrayed his dream.

– And Frances?

– Mother lived alone in the suburbs, taking walks in the park, growing larger. That was when she started writing again.

– Those stories?

– Yes. A couple of little magazines began to publish them. They were intrigued. She developed quite a cult-following after a while.

– Didn't she find literary success irksome?

– It was only a tiny success. A handful of stories dotted about in obscure journals. And, after all, they were all just little empty circles. She didn't pretend she had a story to tell.

– She found her *métier*, at last?

– She liked being alone, drawing circles on blank paper.

– And you, when you were born?

– Well, wasn't I what she had always been waiting for? Her ultimate refusal, come to life? Almost to life. What a pair we were, I was the joke she played on the world.

– Ha ha.

– More?

– If there is more.

– Not much. Scared?

– If the end is nigh, the end is nigh. At least we're both prepared for it. Let's have the rest.

FRANCES TOOK THE baby around the local park every afternoon.

She knew the simple tale her coming and going told the onlooker. The park-keepers had seen her daily throughout her pregnancy and registered her gradually swelling belly. Then a gap, a fortnight's absence, and her return one afternoon flat-stomached, with a pram.

The narrative was so clear, like the wordless series of line-drawings psychologists present to children to test intelligence and personality traits. Only the over-imaginative and disturbed ones would elaborate the story beyond its common meaning. She was concealed by the unambiguous picture she presented to the strangers of her daily life, and by their willingness to see it so. Only the over-imaginative and disturbed would be able to distort the pictures she handed the world into any semblance of the truth. She gained a sharp satisfaction from the discrepancy between the apparent and the real. She enjoyed the deception she played, constantly aware of the public image she portrayed and its distance from the facts of her life; relishing the alternating visions of what they saw and what she knew.

More than that, there was a bitter pleasure, like the shock of crisp, dark chocolate in the mouth, of the possibility of shattering the worlds of those whose first assumptions were normality. One brief sentence from her, and their world would never be quite the same again. They would never again dare to trust the meaning of what they saw. She was potent as a witch with a devastating spell to cast, and every moment of her voluntary silence contained the knowledge of her power. She felt their eyes on her and knew what it was they saw. She granted them her silence; she condemned them to the error of their assumptions.

But away from the illusion she sustained daily in the park, she could be unforgiving. In the street, a dark edge of cruelty emerged. Frances pushed Nony to and from the shops in a small, cunning pram that could convert later into a toddler's pushchair, but in this case wouldn't. It never took very long before passing heads were craning in to look at the contents. People may not, on a world statistical basis, be kindly or concerned about their fellow man, but on a local, passing-in-the-street sort of basis they remain interested in the newborn. A leftover, perhaps, from a tribal past. People do peer into prams and are pleased to see a pink-cheeked infant lying there, rather than the week's supply of potatoes. It was almost invariable. There was hardly a walk that passed without a strange face bearing down and shutting out the sunlight. Not that Nony minded: she didn't distinguish between light and shade. The conversation was invariable too.

'Is that a baby you've got there?'

Frances would smile slightly.

'Oh, yes. Isn't she a pretty one? It is a little girl, isn't it? Yes, I thought so, you can always tell, can't you? *Aren't* you a pretty girl? Yes, you *are*. You're going to be a real heartbreaker when you grow up. I can tell, *yes*, I can. It's those lovely blue eyes.'

Frances would gaze steadily at Nony's admirer until he or she had finished. 'Actually, she can't see.'

The former admirer, overcome with embarrassment, froze, stiff and stuck in the bent-over position of adulation. Frances would go on relentlessly. 'She can't see because she hasn't got any optic nerve. But even if she had, it wouldn't help because she hasn't got a brain for the optic nerve to attach itself to. Her name is Nony,' she would add politely.

Frances waited for them to absorb the meaning of her words, then watched dispassionately as the smug assumptions drained away to be replaced by a rainbow of reactions – fear, sorrow, disgust, anger. It always ended with anger, a searing look of hatred as they lifted themselves straight and walked shakily away.

It *was* cruelty, but it was also a dogged refusal to suppress the truth. Frances told the doters the truth because she didn't see why she should protect them with lies. If they asked, they had to be told. She couldn't see what she owed people that she should have to pretend that things were not as they were, for their benefit. She knew that people felt assaulted by her truth-telling, that they only wanted to admire and congratulate. Why should they have to take on a burden of truth that wasn't theirs? Frances had always had a way of hurting people, of making them feel facile and ridiculous, when all they wanted was to smile and nod well-being in the street. Now she cared less than ever. If they silently assumed the best, she left them to their error; if they asked, they got unvarnished truth. What else was there between silence and the truth? Tact, generosity, gentleness, humanity? All those, of course, but only if you cared enough for life to give those things. Or to have those things to give.

In those first weeks Frances welcomed the baby to the world with a mixture of irony and tenderness that no one had ever, would ever, observe in her. She held Nony in her arms, sang to her, told her stories, and discussed the doings of the world.

'This one's mine,' she said to the rigid-faced nurse in charge of the neo-natal unit, and pointed. 'There's no question of that, is there?' she smiled, picking Nony from her crib to feed her.

There was no need, with Nony, for cruelty or distance, there being no threat or promise in the simple pleasure of handling the soft, warm fellow creature. Nony was hardly to be distinguished from the limp dolls the nurses used to show mothers how to wash and handle their new-born offspring. But she was warm, and a pulse beat through the veins of her forehead. And she was Frances's child.

The biology went on working, combining with the hazard-free nature of the enterprise to surprise Frances with her capacity for tenderness. Her arms ached, the muscles actually straining to take the infant in her arms. They felt incomplete when the silent bundle lay solitary in her crib. Her arms seemed to reach out, almost of their own volition, to pick her up and fill the cradling space between them and Frances's breast. Before Nony, that space had not existed, was no more than the air around her. Now it existed as an incomplete shape, a gap to be filled. Her palm needed the curve of Nony's skull or cheek beneath it; all the other activities of her hand were done to free them from the need to do anything else. Her eyes strained to see the child, compelling her to get up from whatever she was doing and approach Nony's cot, just to look, simply to feast her eyes.

Hormones, Frances knew, but, even so, found herself astonished at their power. She couldn't will herself not to want to have Nony close to her. Once they were at home, alone together, there was no need to try. She allowed her senses all the pleasure they craved. Why not, there was no damage to be done to either of them? Nony wasn't staying. She had nothing to fear from the future, no anxiety that too much, too little, or the inappropriate would alter the blank page she held in her arms. There was nothing that could be written on it. Nony wasn't going to become; no person would struggle through, weighed down with the burden of memory and experience. There would be no repercussions.

And for Frances there would be none of the minuscule, accumulating losses to be borne. No pain at the sight of her child struggling with first sorrows, incomprehensions, disappointments. No equivocal pride at first steps, new schools, the coming to terms with separation. Nony arrived brainless into the world and guaranteed them both an absence of pain.

Sometimes, in the morning when Frances woke her, she licked the sleep from the corners of Nony's eyes, gently with the tip of her tongue, like a queen cat tending her kitten.

'How clever of you,' Frances would smile at the small, silent creature in her arms. 'How simple and easy life can be.'

While Nony slept Frances wrote her stories. She had been contacted by an agent who had suggested putting a book together. Now a contract waited to be signed. It lay for three weeks on the kitchen table. Somehow, Frances was too busy with Nony or writing to get round to finding an envelope and stamp.

'Yes,' she said, when the agent called asking for it. 'I'll sign it today and send it off.' But she always waited for tomorrow.

At six weeks she returned to the hospital for a routine check-up. The incision wound had healed well. An internal examination was part of the routine, along with swabs and a smear.

A fortnight later a letter arrived asking her to attend another appointment. The smear had been positive. Further tests were needed, the letter said, but she was not to be alarmed.

'When did you last have a smear?' the doctor asked.

Frances shook her head. She never had, she had never thought about it.

When the results of the biopsy came through she saw the consultant again. Cervical cancer was well developed, there was a strong possibility that it had spread. She would have to come in for investigation. An operation, chemotherapy. The doctor offered her guarded optimism about her chances of survival, provided they dealt with it immediately.

Frances listened to the information in silence. The doctor noticed the ghost of a smile on her face. He felt as if he were telling her a piece of gossip that she knew about already.

'You understand the seriousness of your condition.'

'Yes, I do,' she nodded. 'What if you don't operate?'

'You might live for no more than a few months. But,' he added reassuringly, 'we'll do whatever we can. Cancer can be quite survivable these days. With our skills and your determination I think you have a good chance.'

Frances dropped her head and bit her upper lip to prevent the smile from widening. The doctor understood her response differently.

'Whatever you do, you mustn't despair. I know it's a terrible shock. Don't hold your feelings in, they're only natural. But we will do everything we can. There *is* hope.' He lifted the receiver of the phone on his desk. 'I'll arrange a bed for you immediately. I see you have a baby. Can the father look after . . .' As he glanced through the notes the nature of the baby's condition came clear to him. 'It's . . . brain-damaged?' He stared at Frances, embarrassed and confused.

Frances nodded.

'No, the father isn't around. Please don't arrange for a bed. I don't want an operation. Thank you, all the same.'

She stood up abruptly. She didn't want a discussion. The consultant tried to stop her.

'Mrs Laughton . . .'

But she had left the room.

The consultant called his secretary.

'Get hold of the hospital social worker and ask her to come and see me, please.'

The woman was clearly in shock. It was not unnatural, and her circumstances were worse than most. He began to read through the paediatric notes, shaking his head. The social worker must get round immediately, and he would contact her doctor. He called admissions and arranged for an emergency bed to be available for the following day. Then he sat quietly for a few moments. Some people, there was no doubt, had extraordinarily bad luck.

Frances sat at the kitchen table with Nony in the crook of her arm. She sipped at the cup of coffee she held in her free hand. She felt serene. The last few weeks had provided a calm that she seemed to have been waiting for all her life, but she had known in the back of her mind that it could only last as long as Nony did. What would happen then she hadn't thought, but she knew that inevitably it would involve the world again. She glanced at the contract lying on the table, and pulled it towards her.

I can sign it now, she thought. The date of publication was projected for nine months ahead. She had been waiting, she realized. Now the last piece of the puzzle had clicked into place. How perfect, how sensible everything was. How right.

She remembered the place that she had gone to as a child, the deep space inside herself where she was herself. When that had gone, closed her out, she had been set adrift. She had become like her parents, waiting the time away. She had been empty and mentally filled herself with bone and muscle.

'But you were there, all along, weren't you?' She looked down at Nony who responded by having one of her muscle spasms. The tension stretched the muscles around her mouth into the rictus of a smile. The small girl in her arms grinned up at her mother. Frances stroked her red hair. She didn't feel empty any more. She never had been; it was only that she had been excluded. It had all been there, waiting, right from the very beginning, from before the beginning. Nothing *did* go on for ever; the end had been built in from the start, in the patterning of the first cell. There was a continuity, a complete circle. She grinned back at Nony, increasing the pressure of her arms around the child.

'Like mother, like daughter,' she whispered.

She would let the cancer grow and bloom inside her like a flower, filling the space that Nony had evacuated. Time was running out for all of them; they would reach their conclusion. Everything would be all right.

– Nony? Are you still there?

  – Yes.

  – The story's finished?

  – Yes.

  – And you're still with us?

  – Yes.

  – What do we do now? Nony?

  – I'm here.

  – We seem to have some time on our hands.

  – Not much. The ending took a lot out of me.

  – It's a sad ending.

  – On the contrary, everyone lives happily ever after. Anyway, it's the same ending as everyone else has.

  – I don't think most people would find it a happy ending.

  – What could be a happier ending than getting what it is you want without even having to try?

  – I grant it was neat. A neat ending, but not a convincing one, I'm afraid.

  – Oh, why not?

  – You're not as up on oncology as you are on anhydranencephalitis. The cancer's ~~too sudden, too far~~ advanced. The woman had just had a Caesarean. Someone would have picked it up. The timing's all wrong.

  – The NHS isn't what it was, you know.

  – Still, it didn't strike me as true.

  – True? I said I'd tell you a story. Did I say anywhere, at any point, that I was going to tell you the truth? I didn't say anything about the truth.

  – You said it was your mother's story, Frances's story.

  – Yes. It's Frances's story.

  – So it's possible there was no malignancy, and that she didn't die.

– Look, what do you want? I told you a story. You wanted a beginning, a middle, and end. You got it.

– Perhaps there was no anhydranencephalic child either.

– It's finished. OK? The story's over.

– But still, if there was no child, no tumour, what would Frances be doing, still alive and without her brainless baby?

– Waiting.

– Waiting?

– For the end. That's all there is to wait for.

– And telling a story to pass the time?

– Yes.

– Her story?

– There isn't any other story to tell.

– She has a lot to thank you for.

– How do you mean?

– For telling her story for her, and giving it a shape. For staying with her through it until the end. For loving her, and letting her love you back.

– Time to fade away, do you think?

– I think so. I think it'll be all right now.

– Thanks for listening.

– It's what I'm here for. Thanks for the story.

– Do you want to tell me something?
– Yes.
– Yes?
– I want to tell you a story.
– A story?
– My story. It's the only one I know.
– Go ahead, I'm listening.